I0596062

A Fatal Folly

A Provincetown Mystery

Jeannette de Beauvoir

HOMEPORT PRESS

A Fatal Folly: A Provincetown Mystery
Copyright © 2019 by Jeannette de Beauvoir

Published by HomePort Press
PO Box 1508
Provincetown, MA 02657
www.HomePortPress.com

ISBN   978-1-7340533-0-2
eISBN 978-1-7340533-1-9

Cover Design by Miladinka Milic

A Fatal Folly is a work of fiction. Other than those individuals who have given their permission and certain well-known landmarks, all names, characters, places, situations, and incidents are the products of the author's imagination and used fictitiously. Any other resemblance to actual events, or persons, living or dead, is purely coincidental.

Also By
Jeannette de Beauvoir

Mysteries:

The Sydney Riley mystery series:

Death of a Bear

Murder at Fantasia Fair

The Deadliest Blessing

A Killer Carnival

The Martine LeDuc series:

Deadly Jewels

Asylum

The Trinity Pierce series:

Murder Most Academic (as Alicia Stone)

Historical Fiction:

Lethal Alliances

Our Lady of the Dunes

1

"I didn't wake you, Sydney, did I?"

The voice on the other and of the telephone was my mother's, and of *course* she'd woken me, it was oh-dark-thirty on a frigid November morning. The heating in my small apartment was on the fritz again and I'd slept under a mountain of comforters that had done nothing to comfort me. Her call didn't exactly improve the situation.

Up in New Hampshire, my mother had probably already finished a load of laundry, caught up with the news on television, made my father an incredibly unhealthy breakfast, watered all her plants, and was now standing in her pristine showroom kitchen, recessed lights blazing, wondering whose life she could disrupt next.

Um, over here? That would be mine.

I struggled onto one elbow. I didn't even want to look at the clock. "Ma, what do you *think*?"

"I always say, start the day with a purpose and you'll get more done," she said. My mother should have been a Marine drill instructor. What am I saying? Marine drill instructors could learn a thing or two from her. I won't go into my childhood; I've already spent too many thousands of dollars in therapy talking about it. "What do you want, Ma?"

"Have you looked at the calendar?" she demanded.

I sighed and burrowed back down under the covers. "Not in the last five minutes," I said.

"Don't take an attitude with me," she snapped. "You always take an attitude with me, Sydney. There's no call for that. And we have to make plans. Christmas will be here before you know it."

Not a chance of that happening; not with my mother in charge. "Ma, it's…" I took my smartphone away from my ear and peered at it. Groaned. "It's not even six o'clock," I said. *Who calls people before six o'clock?*

"I suppose," she said, "you're going to tell me you're too busy to come home for Christmas."

Yes: I'm too busy to come home for Christmas. I plan to be too busy to come home for Christmas for the rest of my life. I'd rather give up a kidney than go home for Christmas, partake of the guilt and remorse my mother regularly serves up along with the turkey and the caroling. Not to mention the level of control she exerts. You don't seriously think my father, retired now for three years, really *wants* bacon and eggs and sausages at five-thirty in the morning, do you? Of course not: my mother wants to serve it, so he has to eat it. I could hear the echo of previous Christmases in my mind. "No, no, don't open your present *that* way, *this* is the right way. We want to save that ribbon!"

If there were nothing else on earth to do, I'd be too busy to come home for Christmas. "Ma, I can't—"

She sniffed. "I knew it. I knew you wouldn't. It's because of *him*," she said darkly, "isn't it?"

Oh, God. I groaned again. "Him" was my boyfriend, Ali, who is second-generation Lebanese-American, and Muslim. My mother acts like he's a terrorist. Well, he *does* work for ICE, and some would consider them terrorists, but he's in human trafficking. As in, trying to stop it.

Not very long ago, Ali was shot. He wasn't working for ICE at the time; he was here in Provincetown, at the inn where I work, investigating something dark and dangerous on his own. For a very short, very terrifying time, I thought he wasn't going to live. They got the bullet out and now he has one hell of a scar, but I still have *him*, and that's really all that counts. That night, leaning against the wall in the hospital corridor, shredding a Styrofoam cup, I'd faced the thought of life without Ali, and I could barely imagine it. I didn't want to imagine it. "What I tell you three times is true," we'd teased each other, and before he went in for surgery he'd told me, three times, that he loved me. I'd had to bend over to hear him.

My mother hadn't been exactly a tower of strength while he was in the hospital, and had ignored his existence since he'd come out of it.

Besides, Ali has nothing to do with my not wanting to go to New Hampshire for Christmas. First of all, there's my mother. Second of all, there's the fact that no matter how my mother phrases it, "home" hasn't been my parents' house for over a decade; home is my own postage-stamp-sized apartment where I live very happily with my roommate, a cat called Ibsen. Third of all… well, there's my mother.

"I have to work," I said, inspired. Which wasn't entirely true. I'm the wedding coordinator at the Race Point Inn, and while there are generally one or two weddings around Christmas and the New Year, there aren't enough to keep me fully employed, not the way I am in the summer. So I do what everybody else does in this beach resort town in the off-season: I cobble together other things to pay the outrageous rent my landlord requires to keep me in my little place. This year I was working part-time in one of the town's few galleries that keeps some limited wintertime hours, though not a lot of them.

"You're not doing weddings," she said with a triumphant flourish: Hercule Poirot making a surprise announcement after deep detective work.

No," I agreed. "But I'm working all the same. And it's almost Holly Folly."

"Don't be ridiculous, Sydney," she said automatically, and then, almost as an afterthought, "It's almost *what?*"

"Holly Folly." I struggled into a sitting position and pulled the comforters closer around me. I was looking forward to Holly Folly. The dance club I live over is open then, which means my landlord will be paying more attention to the heat situation. "It's a kind of pre-Christmas celebration here in town," I said.

The first time my mother visited me, she took one look at Commercial Street—P'town's main drag—then turned to me and said, "So, what is it? You're a lesbian now?" People see what they expect to see. The truth is that while we *are* a première gay resort town, neither our visitors nor our residents are actually required to follow that (or any) orientation.

Holly Folly, on the other hand, is an unabashed LGBTQ holiday celebration. Everyone's invited and welcome, but it's not everyone's idea of a jolly Currier and Ives etching. Oh, there are Christmas trees, and carols sung around various pianos, and plenty of mulled cider and buttered rum; but there's also the Santa Speedo race down Commercial Street, the concert by the Boston Gay Men's Chorus, and drag queens decked out as everything from angels to Santa's helpers to tinsel-encrusted Christmas trees.

Don't get me wrong: there are aspects of Holly Folly I probably couldn't live without, or at any rate can't imagine Christmas without. There are the most amazing cookies, decorated so delicately you can scarcely believe they're edible, at the Gifford House. There are concerts and singalongs. There's the Shop Hop, with great prizes as well as great prices in all the shops and galleries along Commercial Street, and you can take the trolley between them all for free; and there's the Inn Stroll, an open house at a staggering number of P'town's famed guest houses—including the Race Point Inn—where the innkeepers out-Martha-Stewart each other in decorations, treats, and libations, many of which are decidedly in the adult-beverage category. Staggering is the right word: last year Ali and I went on the Inn Stroll and he had to practically carry me back to the apartment. It's a good thing he's Muslim and doesn't drink alcohol.

My mother interrupted that fond memory. "Well, whatever it is," she said, "Christmas is all about family."

Well, that or joy to the world, I thought. And then I did it. I made one of my most spectacularly appalling mistakes *ever*. I opened my mouth.

"Why don't you come here instead?" I asked.

I ought to be shot.

***

It was Ibsen who finally got me out of bed. He can be extremely persuasive when he's hungry, and whatever time I wake up in the morning is, to his mind, the time he should get fed. "Don't look at me like that," I said crossly. "At least you're wearing a fur coat."

Ibsen was unimpressed. He often is.

I pulled on three layers of clothing and staggered around the kitchen—or the area of my apartment I rather grandly refer to as such—totally on autopilot. Feed the cat. Start the coffee. Leave the first of several messages to Zack, my landlord, about the heat. Try and remember what day it is. Let's face it, you're not getting full competence at six o'clock in the morning in late November. The sun wasn't even going to be up for another hour.

I slumped down at my table and stared into the depths of my as-of-yet empty coffee cup and tried to make out why I'd just invited my mother to come to P'town for the holidays. Usually I only make rash ridiculous invitations like that when I'm solidly drunk, invitations I subsequently can't remember until someone shows up for a dinner I didn't realize I'd invited them to. I didn't even have the benefit of alcohol-induced amnesia here.

She'd said yes, of course. With alacrity. She was probably as startled by the invitation as I was.

I wanted to call someone who might commiserate with my stupidity—or even tell me it was all just a bad dream—but there's no one I know who's awake at six. Ibsen had already been clear about his level of concern. Mirela—my best friend—is a visual artist, a painter in oils, who does the club scene at night and thinks of ten o'clock as breakfast time. Ali was currently in California, working undercover with some sex traffickers. That was, perhaps, the only comforting thought I was holding on to: as much as I hated him being undercover (these are the people, after all, who pretty much routinely get killed), it might mean he'd still be out there when my mother came to visit. Not that Ali has ever been anything but unfailingly polite to her. It was me I was worried about: I might kill her, and then I'd have to go to prison, and that sort of thing really ruins the holidays.

If my mother didn't manage that already.

I considered reading the news on my tablet, but that was too depressing: politicians continued to do one outrageous thing after another, and people agreed it was outrageous, and then everyone moved on. It was too exhausting to even contemplate.

The more immediate world didn't hold a lot of better prospects. It had snowed in the night, and the only thing that was cheering me up was that in four hours I was scheduled to be at the gallery, so there was the prospect of heat in my future. Until then I was pretty much on my own. Far Land Provisions, the only reliable place for coffee off-season, didn't open until seven.

I did the only reasonable thing and went back to bed.

2

Even if you didn't know Holly Folly was coming, you'd know Holly Folly was coming. Or that *something* was happening, anyway. The town had that buzz, the same buzz you start picking up in April when the contractors all arrive to make renovations before the season starts, and shops and restaurants begin opening up again.

It's a little more muted, because of the cold, but the weeks approaching Holly Folly give off that same kind of vibe. There are all the pre-Holly Folly events: the Lighting of the Pilgrim Monument, Thanksgiving, the lighting of the lobster pot tree. By Holly Folly we're as jolly as we get and there's still that week of concerts, parties, and fun.

Mirela was all about it. I stopped by her studio as soon as I was finished at the gallery, and found her surrounded by oils and rags and partially finished canvases; Mirela never does just one painting at a time. She also sells—at least—

five or six during Holly Folly, so she likes to stock up before the holidays actually begin. "I'm busy, sunshine," she informed me when she came to open the door.

"So I see." She had paint all over her smock, tangled in her blonde hair, and a streak of vermilion swept across one cheek—and she *still* looked better than I do on my best days. "I have to talk to you anyway," I said.

She shrugged and went back to work. "Then you can talk," she said.

I looked around for someplace to sit. Mirela has a studio right on the harbor that gets unimaginable light, and she's filled it with stuff—seashells and driftwood, books on art, canvases, jam jars filled with substances of uncertain origin—and every available surface always seems to be taken. I located a stool, swept some paintbrushes and three back issues of the Provincetown Banner off it, and perched. "I asked my parents to come here for the holidays," I said.

That stopped her, all right. She turned to stare at me, palette in one hand, brush in the other. "I have not heard you correctly," she said. "It sounded like you said you invited your parents to come."

I nodded. "I did."

She continued staring. "This is not funny, sunshine," she said.

"I know," I replied, and abandoned all pretense of taking it lightly. "Oh, my God, Mirela, what am I going to do?"

"Why did you do this?"

"I don't *know*!" I wailed. "I was talking with my mother, it was ridiculously early, but that's no excuse, and then suddenly these words are coming out of my mouth and I have no idea where they came from!"

She shook her head. "You're mad," she informed me.

"I know," I said miserably.

She turned back to her canvas. "You can always become sick," she said philosophically.

"Not a chance. My mother knows that trick. She spent my childhood listening to me claim I was sick every time I didn't want to go to school."

She shrugged and dabbed some violent yellow paint on the canvas. "Tell them you do not have space in your apartment. It is the truth, anyway."

"Mirela," I said, "I work at an *inn*. They never expect to stay at my apartment."

She paused, her head on one side, contemplating her work. Mirela's style's evolved considerably since she first came to Provincetown from Bulgaria, one of the waves of students who arrive every summer, work fourteen jobs, share a place with twelve other people, and generally keep the town ticking along every season. A few of them every year find full-time work and housing and stay; Mirela found overnight success as a painter. I had a couple of small pieces she'd done, both of which were gifts; I couldn't dream of affording her prices anymore. In the eight or ten years she'd been in Provincetown she'd gone from fishing boats to much more abstract work. It didn't matter what she did; it all sold.

Now I scowled at the canvas. "What's that supposed to be, anyway?"

"What do you see in it, sunshine?" Mirela thinks "sunshine" is an endearment; I've never had the heart to disabuse her.

"That's a rotten question. It's like asking people, how old do I look? No matter what you say, it's going to be the wrong answer."

"You," she informed me, "are in a mood. You haven't heard from Ali, have you?"

"I'm not supposed to hear from Ali. That's the point of undercover."

It wasn't, of course. Even undercover agents, especially those under for a long time, are able from time to time with proper precautions to be in touch with people from their real lives, especially partners. But I hadn't heard from him in almost two weeks, and your brain does funny things, doesn't it?

Mirela shot me a look. "You are worried," she informed me.

"I'm not."

"You are," she said, nodding vigorously. "You are thinking he could be killed."

"Well, not at that particular moment I wasn't, but thanks for reminding me," I said sourly. The truth was I didn't know how to feel. We'd had a reasonably long-distance relationship—well, Provincetown to Boston—for as long as we'd been together, so on one hand his absence wasn't worrying; I'm old enough to understand I really don't want to be living with anybody, anyway. But I'd recently seen two detective-show reruns (what else do you do on winter nights but get caught up on Netflix and watch reruns?) that showed undercover agents getting killed, and it was all a little upsetting. I didn't know what he was doing, I didn't know where he was doing it, and I didn't know when he'd stop doing it.

Other than that, everything was just fine.

"Anyway," I said to Mirela, "Ali isn't the problem."

"Your mother seems to think he is."

"She'd think anyone was a problem. My mother wants to hand-pick my husband." She shot me a look. "Future husband," I amended. "*Hypothetical* husband."

"Your problem," she pronounced, as if announcing a deep esoteric truth, "is your mother."

"You can say that again." I sighed and pushed myself off the stool. "And you're not being particularly helpful," I added.

"You do not see me inviting *my* parents for the holidays."

"Your parents live in Bulgaria."

"And that is where they will stay," she said, and stood back from the canvas. "Tell me the truth, sunshine. What do you think?"

I fled.

***

I had a text message from my landlord informing me he was working on the heat situation, so I decided to leave him to it. I had to do some grocery shopping, anyway, and Stop & Shop was as good a place as any for self-flagellation over my unfortunate impromptu conversation.

I took my Honda Civic—known to all and sundry merely as the Little Green Car, since I'd been thoroughly unimaginative when I first acquired it and had to come up with a name—gathered my shopping bags (Provincetown is several years into its eco-ban on single-use plastic bags) and headed over. The really great thing about going to Stop & Shop in the winter is that it doesn't give you time to dwell on anything, because it's definitely our communication-central hub. Going through the grocery store, you can catch up with friends, find out who's seeing whom, make a massage appointment, learn about a new yoga class, or commiserate about the dearth of Indian restaurants in town.

You can also, if absolutely necessary, buy groceries.

It was snowing again, which was odd for November–we don't really get anything significant much before the new year—and I had made my way through the produce and fish sections and was trying to decide whether or not to indulge my admittedly childish passion for Cap'n Crunch cereal when my name came over the loudspeaker, asking me to report to customer service. I checked my pockets for wallet, phone, and keys—all there–before heading over. Curiouser and curiouser, as Alice in Wonderland would say. "I'm Sydney Riley, what is it?"

"Oh, Sydney," said the woman there whose name I couldn't right at that moment remember. "I'm sorry—I recognized the description of your car."

"What description of my car?" But I knew, already. The man standing nearby in a black wool Armani coat cleared his throat diffidently. "I'm afraid," he said, "that I've–er–hit it. Your car, that is."

I stared at him blankly. "Okay. Thanks." Wait—I was thanking him for hitting my car? And how hit was it? I amended my tone quickly. "So do you have your insurance papers on you? Mine are in my glove compartment."

"I'm rather afraid that it's going to require more than that," he said.

English accent, blue eyes. Not exactly a harbinger of doom. "What do you mean?"

He glanced at the woman behind the desk, who was listening openly and avidly. "I'm terribly sorry. It's a different vehicle than I'm accustomed to driving, you see, with the left-hand steering and all, and the snow–"

What did you do to my Little Green Car? "I don't understand."

"Perhaps we can go outside and I'll show you."

This wasn't good. This was definitely not good. And it didn't help that nearly everyone I knew–which was nearly everyone in the store—was watching us head out. I wrapped my scarf more closely around my neck. Any day that begins with my mother on the telephone is bound to not end well.

This one clearly wasn't. The whole back left side of the Little Green Car was crumpled, with a big black SUV still lodged against it. He'd tried to stop, clearly, and had slid in the not-yet-plowed new snow. Probably going too fast. It didn't matter; what mattered was I wasn't driving it home. "I'll be happy to take care of everything," the Englishman was saying, his voice brisk. "And a rental car for you in the meantime."

Did he really think there was going to be a rental available in Provincetown in the winter? Who was he, anyway, and what was he doing here? "Who are you, anyway?" I demanded at last. He knew my name; it had been broadcast all over the Stop & Shop.

He cleared his throat. "My name's Guy Husband," he said, and then, as though knowing the reaction that inevitably followed, "It truly is my real name. I'm English."

That was supposed to explain it? "I have AAA," I said. "They'll tow it to the garage." Which was in Orleans; my basic membership wasn't going to cover that. I looked at him speculatively. "It won't be cheap."

"It's all right," he said, waving a gloved hand dismissively. "I'll take care of the cost. Come sit in the warm while we arrange it."

I didn't have a lot of choice. Sitting in the heated SUV–still lodged up against the Little Green Car–I listened to him making telephone calls. "Are you here on vacation?" I asked.

He looked distracted. "Sorry?"

I gestured. "You have a new vehicle you're not used to, and you don't live here. Are you here on vacation?"

"Oh, I see. No. No, not exactly." He half-turned to face me. "Look, I've taken the photos for the insurance companies. I interrupted your shop. Why don't you finish it, and I'll drive you and your parcels home? It's the least I can do, really."

While I secretly agreed, I didn't exactly want to go back in and deal with the commiserations and curiosity of everyone in the store. "It's all right, it can wait," I said automatically, then remembered how cold it was outside. "But if you want to drive me home, that would be all right."

"Of course." He'd apparently already checked that his SUV was in working order; now he put it smoothly into reverse and pulled away from the Little Green Car. I looked out the window at it morosely. It didn't actually look all that bad, now the two vehicles were disconnected, and perhaps it wouldn't be too difficult to get fixed. Unless the frame was bent…

Guy Husband was saying something, and I pulled my attention back to him. "Excuse me?"

"…where you live?"

"On Carver Street." In an apartment where, please God, the heat was working again. I struggled to find the Social Sydney. "What about you? You said you're not exactly on vacation. I haven't seen you around town before."

"I'm staying at the Race Point Inn," he said. "It's on Commercial–"

"I know where it is," I interrupted. "I work there."

"Really?" A quick look. "I haven't seen you around."

"I do wedding and event planning," I said. "Not so much of it in the winter."

He nodded and kept his eyes on the road. "So what do *you* do?" I asked, more for anything to say than out of actual curiosity.

A quick glance. "Have you heard of Robert Whittier?"

I stared at him. "Everyone's heard of Robert Whittier," I said. At least, everyone on the Cape who's remotely involved in tourism, or marine science, or boating... Robert Whittier is an underwater archaeological explorer best known for discovering the remains of Samuel "Black Sam" Bellamy's wrecked pirate ship Whydah, the only fully verified pirate ship-wreck from the Golden Age of Piracy. Which just happened to have sunk in a bad nor'easter right off the tip of Cape Cod.

Whittier found it, dived it, and the exploration continues every year. There are two muse-ums on the Cape filled with pirate lore and Whydah artifacts, one of them on MacMillan Pier in Provincetown. The Whydah is one of our claims to fame; everyone on the Cape feels a certain ownership of the story.

"Well," he said, slowing down for a cross-street, "the Whydah wasn't the only ship that went down that night. Bellamy had a whole fleet." He glanced across at me. "You know who Bellamy—"

I didn't let him finish. "Everyone knows who Bellamy is," I snapped.

"So there you are," he said comfortably. He didn't seem to find me off-putting, which was a bit of a novelty; most people aren't crazy about the sarcasm. "He had a whole fleet heading to Maine when the storm hit. The Whydah was the flagship, the one he captained. There was an-other ship, a French sloop they'd captured off Cuba, that same spring of 1716, called the Mi-gnonette. She was probably sailing close to the Whydah and went down at the same time, not too far away from the Whydah, somewhere this side of Race Point."

"Okay," I said, though this was all news to me. Not to mention captain as a verb. "So where do *you* come in?"

He pulled cautiously onto Bradford Street. "Well, that's just it," he said. "I'm trying to beat Robert Whittier to the Mignonette."

3

I have a confession to make: I don't get my car serviced in P'town. We have several decent garages, independently owned, etc., etc., and I commit the combined deadly sins of going out of town and to a garage that's part of a national chain. I can't help it: I happened accidentally (quite literally, but that's a story for another time) upon Midas in Orleans, three towns away from Provincetown, and John and Dave have gone above and beyond taking good care of me and the Little Green Car ever since.

Guy Husband assured me he'd pay for the tow. He was anxious about making the arrangements, anxious too—having effectively aborted my grocery run—that I had enough to eat at home. We sat in his SUV figuring out all the details. I was in no hurry to go upstairs; I had no idea whether or not heat had been restored, and if it hadn't, it was going to be a long night.

Besides that, of course, I was enthralled by his presence in town, if only because no one else knew about it. I was quite sure of that: if anyone knew, Mirela would, and she hadn't breathed a word to me. To get the inside scoop before Mirela was one hell of a feat. Besides that, it was fascinating.

"There were rumors another ship went down," he was saying.

"I've never heard them," I said. "And I hear all the rumors." Not quite true, but close enough.

"Not *now*." He looked at me as though re-assessing my intelligence. "Then. When it happened. Everyone was talking about it."

"And you overheard them?"

He was starting to get a sense of who I was, and the next step, I knew by long experience, was going to be irritation. "People wrote about it," he said patiently. "In ships-sighted logs. In port journals. In correspondence. One does *research*."

One does? "So who was on the Mignonette?" I asked.

"I'm rather less concerned with the who than I am with the what," he said, looking out through the windshield. The wipers were set to intermittent and the street seemed to blur between swipes, making it all soft and gentle and pretty, an impressionist painting in shades of gray. He twisted in the seat to look at me, an eyebrow raised. "Pirate treasure," he said.

"Pieces of eight?" I knew it wouldn't be; that was Spanish currency, and while there might have been some of it mixed in with the fleet's take, pieces of eight were more along the lines of Captain Jack Sparrow than Captain Sam Bellamy. Pirates probably didn't celebrate Talk Like A Pirate Day, either. Real life is so disillusioning.

"It's not about the actual value," he said. "It's the scientific value. It's finding out more, learning what we didn't know, exposing people to a different time and a different life. That's the real treasure. It's understanding that pirates lived a pretty decent life, all in all." He smiled. "Every taking was split evenly among the men. They were completely at ease with being multi-ethnic—there's only one recorded pirate ship that didn't have black or Native American crew. They played dice on board. Every man on board got the same cut of whatever they made. They—" He cut himself off.

There was a pause. "*You* used to teach school," I said, nodding knowingly.

"Once upon a time. Was I that priggish?"

I shrugged. "Not really. It's interesting, anyway," I said. Of course it was interesting: who doesn't like a pirate story? Every summer, people flock to the two Whydah museums for a reason. The stories are in our shared consciousness, our collective unconscious, something like that. Jung would probably have a lot to say about it all.

"It's what I do," he said somberly. "It's all I've ever been interested in doing, diving wrecks. Finding history. Telling stories. It's all I'm really good at."

Nice work if you can get it, I thought; but you have to have more than just an interest and mad research skills to mount Robert Whittier-sized expeditions. "How are you paying for it?"

He was looking out at the snow again. "I own a marine salvage company," he said, and you could tell his mind was somewhere else, and not just on sunny beaches or calm seas. Something about that company bothered him; there was some shadow, some unfinished business. He roused himself and his mind came back to the SUV. "That's how I started out. One small leaky vessel working the Channel, out there in all weather, out there when I was sick and tired of being out there, and built it up from that point. I moved up to a better vessel, and then another, and then another." He glanced at me. "You have to understand, I'm no pirate, and no thief. Anything abandoned or sunk offshore is fair game. I built the company up slowly and I've been quite extraordinarily lucky. I've got investors, of course, who doesn't? But I'm the major one; most of it's my money." He let a small smile slip. "If I could have seen into the future! Now I own a research marine company with a hundred employees and three ships and more electronic equipment than you'll see anywhere outside of Woods Hole."

Woods Hole Oceanographic Institute, that was, the owners of the submersible Alvin, explorers of the world's seas. Also located on the Cape. We're just a hotbed of marine science. I cleared my throat. "I'm impressed," I admitted. And it *was* impressive… as far as it went. "I'm just seeing one flaw in your plan."

That eyebrow again. "Just one?"

I gestured out the windshield. "You got your hemisphere and timing wrong. This isn't exactly diving weather."

He relaxed and laughed. "No," he agreed. "Not even close. We're not going down anywhere until spring."

"So," I said, "you're here now because…?"

He smiled. "Now *that* would be telling," he said. "And I've been boring you far too long with my story. Let me apologize again for the circumstances that brought us together, Ms. Riley."

The conversation was clearly over. "Okay," I said slowly.

"If you're sure you have everything you need for this evening," he said, "I'll just ring you in the morning to get your rental vehicle to you."

"Okay," I said again. I was a little bewildered. "Thanks."

He inclined his head. I fumbled for the latch, opened the door, and spilled myself out of the SUV. God, these things were tall. "I'll talk to you tomorrow."

"Good-bye, Ms. Riley."

I went up the stairs, muttering something peevish and adolescent about being dismissed. Only the English, I thought, could do it so elegantly. And pirate stories aside, you had to admit, it hadn't been the best possible day. I didn't even know which of my problems was worse, my mother or my car. I just knew it was getting dark, it was very cold, and I wasn't in the mood. If I didn't have heat…

If I didn't have heat, I thought suddenly, I would march straight down to the Race Point Inn, throw myself on the mercy of its owner—my boss, Glenn—and demand a room. No matter how hysterical I had to be to get it, it's what I'd do. There was just so much a girl could take in one day.

I noticed several things when I opened my door: the heat was on, and so was the light. Ibsen was purring so loudly I could hear it across the room, and my friend John was asleep on my sofa.

I wonder if other women live normal lives.

***

I scrounged supper from the freezer. I had some lasagna I'd made the week before, and there was some Romaine lettuce that wasn't completely wilted, and of course I always have an emergency bottle of Côtes du Rhone around. Even in an apartment the size of mine, you can't get through life without an emergency bottle of Côtes du Rhone.

John stirred and yawned and gradually returned to the land of the living as I was heating the lasagna in the oven; the smell probably woke him. I sat in the one comfortable chair I own and watched him.

He opened an eye. "Oh, hey, Sydney."

"Hello, John." Ibsen jumped up on my lap and settled in, flexing his claws right through my jeans. "Ouch. Nice to see you."

"Uh-huh." He struggled to a sitting position. I have a very old sofa and it tends to do a Little Shop of Horrors act with anyone who sits in it; it's hard to extricate oneself.

I grabbed Ibsen's paws so he'd stop stabbing me. "Stop that! Staying to dinner, John?"

"Zack had me over looking at your heat."

I immediately felt kindlier toward him. "You're the one who fixed it! You wonderful man!" Of course the landlord wasn't going to hire a company to come look at it, not when he could do it on the cheap with a handyman like John. Still, I didn't care as long as the damned thing worked.

He nodded, elbows on knees, still waking up. "Uh-huh."

"Then I definitely owe you dinner," I said.

He peered at me long enough that I wondered if he was doing drugs again. For a surprising number of people out here at Land's End, sobriety is definitely a one day at a time matter, and long cold desolate lonely winters don't help with those twelve grueling steps. "Okay," he said at last.

I decanted Ibsen onto the floor and headed over to the area I like to call my kitchen. "You like lasagna?"

"I like everything." He was scratching his head. "You going to the Lighting?"

"I always go to the Lighting." Everyone does; even though tourists have been known to ask what we do with the Pilgrim Monument in the off-season (surely that has to be apocryphal, people couldn't really be that dense), it dominates the town year-round, and toward the end of November special lights strung from the top to the base are lit and stay on until the new year—in addition to its usual lighting. They're bright and festive and can be seen the moment you come over the Truro hill on Route Six. There's an official ceremony, with speeches from local dignitaries, and a countdown, followed by music and hot cider and cookies in the museum at the base of the monument. If you live in P'town, you go to the Lighting.

"Used to be colored," John said. "The lights? Did you know that?"

I checked the lasagna and put more time on the microwave. "No. What's the story?"

He nodded, settling into it. John's an old-timer, Provincetown born and bred, and likes to know things the rest of us—known locally as washashores—aren't aware of. "Used to be colored lights," he said again. "Now they're all white."

Okay; there could have been a story there, but not in John's telling. I poured two glasses of water from the filter pitcher in the fridge and put them on the table along with plates and silverware and napkins.

He roused himself; he'd seen the bottle I put on the counter. "You can have wine," he said. "Don't bother me. Never liked it much anyway." It was true: when John drank, it had been Miller Lights, pounding them down by the six-pack, something I'd never understand in a thousand years. I poured myself a modest half-glass and set it by my place. "So what have you been up to, besides fixing my heat, for which I'm eternally grateful?"

He shrugged and shambled over to the table. "Down the beach," he said. When John isn't working—and there's a lot less call for what he does in the off-season—he wanders around scouring the Outer Cape for stuff. Some of what he finds he donates to the thrift shop at the Methodist church on Shank Painter, some of it he barters, most of it he takes into his workshop and crafts into clever objects he sells to shops on Commercial Street that in turn charge about three hundred percent more than they paid John—and get it. Tourists like one-of-a-kind seaside-themed curios.

I put the salad, such as it was, on the table. "What'd you find?"

He emptied his pockets, which really wasn't what I'd had in mind, what with the accompanying sand. Beach glass—lots of it; November's great for stuff like that, with the high tides and winds and storms we get. There isn't much people haven't found washed up in November. A couple of small pieces of twisted wood. A whole lot of coins, some of them foreign; he likes those, puts them around frames or mirrors and polyurethanes the hell out of it, the result is really quite pretty and what they call a conversation piece.

I served the lasagna and sat down. Took a sip of wine. And just for something to do—like, starting a conversation—I poked through the coins.

And found something that changed everything.

4

J ohn was watching me.

"You knew this was here, didn't you?" I asked rhetorically. His expression already told me what I needed to know; he'd been waiting for me to see it. "Damn, John, I never noticed your flair for the dramatic before."

He just smiled.

I held it in my hand reverently, like gold. Never mind the likeness: gold was exactly what I was holding. A lost dream, stolen and sought and stolen again, smudged and dirty on the ocean floor. Worn and chipped—can gold be chipped?—and hard to read, but gold for all of that. I'd seen the fake coins they give kids at the pirate museum, and this wasn't one of them. Not even close. I imagined the handsome Sam Bellamy clinking it in his pocket. "The last person who touched this…" I breathed.

"…was me," said John, always prosaic.

I looked at him, the pieces clicking in my head. Still, I had to be sure. Too much of a coincidence otherwise. "Did you know there's a guy in town—"

"—named Guy? I'm the one brought him here." He was watching me watch him, and was looking pretty smug about it for a moment: a major achievement, that, John as rocker of worlds. Then he shrugged and pointed to my hand. "Well, okay, not me, it was that thing brought him here. But I'm the one told him about it."

"How?"

"I *called* him? Sent him a *picture*?" Sometimes he sounds like an adolescent girl or a Canadian, John does, sentences ending as potential questions. "Came off the beach last weekend, after that nor'easter? That an' a bunch more stuff I found. Told him about it, and next thing I know, he's flying in. Not even Cape Air; got his own plane, can you believe that?"

"Where d'you find it?" Okay, I knew he wasn't telling, but I had to ask.

He tapped his nose.

I frowned. "Tapping your nose? What's that supposed to mean?"

"Means I'm keeping it to myself, for now," he said. "No sense sending every treasure-hunter on the East Coast out after it."

"Just Guy Husband," I said. There was probably a hefty finder's fee involved; I wouldn't be surprised. "What I don't understand is why no one's been talking about this boat before."

"Ship," said John. "It's not a boat. It was a sloop."

Okay, here's the thing. I've taken the Baystate Cruise Company's fast ferry to and from Boston. I've done the sunset sail around the harbor on each of the town's two schooners, the Hindu and the Bay Lady. I've even once or twice rented a nineteen-foot sailboat from Flyers Marine and careened madly about with my friend Thea and way too many wine spritzers. That was the full extent of my nautical knowledge. "Okay, then, sloop," I said, undeterred. "Why hasn't everyone been talking about it?"

"It's tidewrack," he said, shrugging. "Jetsam. Plenty of it to find. You know what they call the Cape." He took a large bite of lasagna. "Hey, this is good!"

"Don't sound so surprised," I said, sourly. And I *do* know what they call the Cape: before they built the Cape Cod Canal for safer access, the coast was known as the graveyard of the Atlantic, with something ridiculous like over three thousand documented wrecks… and who knew how many more were there, nameless ships, faceless victims, mysterious cargoes. Then in the early 1900s sometime—I'm fuzzy on the details, I keep thinking I'll take the canal tour, and then I don't—they put in the canal so no one has to round Race Point or go near the Peaked Hill Bars or any of the other coastal dangers.

Every winter storm—and we have plenty of them—that used to claim the ships now dug their debris from the sandy bottom and flung it up onshore. You never knew what you were going to find after a nor'easter.

I'd never seen anything like this, though. I frowned. "It *could* be from the Whydah," I said.

John shook his head, washed down another enormous bite of lasagna with his water, and cleared his throat. "Not a chance," he said. "Whittier's got the site wrapped up. Besides, wrong beach."

"Which beach?"

"Sydney," John said, "I like you a lot."

"But not that much," I said, smiling. "I get it. But you called in Guy Husband, so you had to be pretty sure. Who is he, anyway? How did you know who to call?" Or was it whom to call?

"Got a company, Marine Preservation and Salvage? Something like that." John shrugged, nonchalant, like he was admitting to having partied with Jagger or Richards back in the day. "I know a guy worked with him off Scotland one year. Somebody I trust. Good guy." Another drink of water. "Thought it was worth a look. So he talked to Guy Husband, and he looked at some pictures I took of the thing, and then he thought it was a good idea to come on over himself. In his own private jet." He said it reverently.

I was still examining the coin. "Wait," I said. "You said sloop. Sloop, right? You know what this is from, don't you?" I remembered the warmth in the SUV, the heated seats, Guy Husband's eyes on the road. "This is from the Mignonette!"

John nodded, unimpressed with my knowledge. He was busy scraping his plate.

I stared at the coin some more. How did they connect all this with a ship that sank in a storm—how long ago? Two and a half centuries? It made sense there was a fleet—I'd never given the matter any thought, to be perfectly honest, but that made sense, if you were attacking ships on the high seas you'd at least want to outnumber them—but how did people know which ship was which, and which ones were lost, and where, and… it was all fascinating and so far outside my areas of expertise to be completely baffling. "How do they do it?"

He pushed himself back from the table and wiped his mouth on his napkin. "That was really good, thanks, Sydney." He held out his hand for the coin. "Research," he said. "They pretty much know what's where down there, I think? Stuff like this just narrows it down. It wasn't like I was telling him anything new. More like I was showing him it was real?" It was one of the longest speeches I'd ever heard from John; he must be feeling strongly about this.

I handed the coin back reluctantly. "Thanks for showing it to me."

He ducked his head in response, stood up, and shoved it back in his pocket. "Guy's in town," he said.

"I know," I said. "He hit my car at the Stop & Shop."

He looked startled. Apparently his grapevine had failed him here. "You okay?"

"I'm fine, but the Little Green Car needs some work," I said. "He's bringing me a rental in the morning."

"Good." He shrugged himself into his coat. "Okay, that's all. Your heat should be fine now."

"Thanks, John," I said fervently. "That's the best pre-Christmas present ever." Testing his sense of humor, I added, "Better even than pirate treasure from the Mignonette."

"Don't you believe it. Nothin' better than pirate treasure," he said, and was gone.

I stacked the dishes in the sink and ran hot water on them, thinking. So even if all these people did their research and found out where a ship was, or where they thought a ship was—what the hell was Guy Husband doing in Provincetown in November? We can barely swim on the backshore in *August*, the water's that cold—it's the Labrador Current going by, don't kid yourself—so why was he here now? John could have just sent him the artifact for him to examine, ponder over, prepare.

Something else was going on.

The phone rang and I dried my hands hurriedly and peered at the display. My boss at the Race Point Inn. "Glenn," I said.

"Hey, Sydney." I could picture him, sitting comfortably in his suite of rooms off the reception area, a big bear of a man, sipping some ancient brandy. In his case, the expression is literal: Glenn is what is known as a bear, a large hairy gay man fond of food, good company, and other big hairy gay men. Like most bears, he's one of the sweetest people around. "We've got a couple here thinking of getting married at Holly Folly."

"Terrific." I switched ears so I could grab a notepad; switched mental gears, too. "Tell me more."

"Thought you might come by tomorrow if you're not working at the gallery. You can talk to them then, or at least I can update you," he said. "Just find me when you get there, have a couple of things to go over with you."

"Sure." I had no idea what the next day would bring besides a rental car, Guy Husband, and some hours at the gallery, but I'd work it out. "Can I call you in the morning to confirm? I had a fender-bender today and need to deal with that first."

"You okay?" It was nice that everyone was concerned.

"Fine. The Little Green Car, not so much."

"Do what you need to do," Glenn said. "I'll talk to you in the morning."

"Okay. 'Night, boss."

I sighed and opened a can of cat food: back to the prosaic details of life. It was fun thinking about pirate treasure; who didn't have a little kid inside them who'd wanted to be a pirate? I didn't have to close my eyes for it to come surging over me, the sheer reckless delight of endless summer days, days so sweet you could crunch them in your mouth. The porch railing at my parents' home, the tricornered hats left over from some Fourth of July fancy-dress party, a wooden sword I'd made with my father in his workshop back when he still liked doing that sort of thing, painted silver and, to my eyes, stunning and dangerous.

The porch was the deck; Lily and Peter and I were the Pirates of Leominster Road, out for a long hot day of sailing the seven seas and screaming "Avast!" at every child—or rabbit— that hove into view. The smell of cooking coming from the house, rich herbs and mushrooms, but we were far away, off toward India or China, ready to pounce upon the rich merchant ships littering the sea, ready to make our names and our fortunes. My mother's voice, calling me in to dinner, Lily and Peter drifting off to their own homes in the twilight, my shining sword turning back into a handmade piece of useless wood.

I shook myself; that had been fun, for sure. I'd almost forgotten us. The Pirates of Leominster Road. I'd much prefer to think about that.

Much more fun than current Real Life, remembering there'd been a time when I'd been able to hold Real Life at bay and become a pirate. Much more fun than wondering what was happening with Ali out in California, or what the hell I was going to do about my parents coming for Christmas, or what might be wrong with my car. I put all those things firmly out of my mind and curled up on my sofa with a glass of wine, my cat, and my laptop.

I knew approximately what most Cape Cod residents know about Black Sam Bellamy. Time to learn a little more.

"Fight smart, harm few, score big" seemed to summarize the Bellamy strategy. He lived it, too: he didn't engage in wholesale slaughter. Took what he wanted and said thank you. Centuries ago, he'd dreamt of a world in which people could respect each other, in which fairness was more than a luxury, in which every voice was heard. We hadn't managed to make Sam Bellamy's vision a reality in the twenty-first century, and we were heading away from it at breakneck speed. But what really struck me was his age. When the Whydah went down, Sam was only twenty-eight years old.

When I was twenty-eight, I could hardly think my way out of a paper bag with a machete; this guy had commanded a fleet of ships.

And had done it—dare I say—nicely. There's no record of him ever killing a captive, and he often returned captured ships and cargo if they didn't suit his purpose. Ships that *did* suit his purpose were definitely moving up on the moral compass: the Whydah and the Mignonette had both been slave traders, part of the horrible dark Atlantic Circle that kept plantations and slavers alike profitable.

The first side of the triangle was the export of goods from Europe to Africa. A number of African kings and merchants took part in the trading of enslaved people; it was almost comforting to me that we in America hadn't invented the practice. Perfected it, maybe. For each captive, the African rulers would receive a variety of stuff from Europe, including guns, ammunition, and other factory-made goods. The second leg of the triangle exported enslaved Africans across the Atlantic Ocean to the Americas and the Caribbean islands. The third and final part of the triangle was the return of goods to Europe from the Americas. The goods were the products of slave-labor plantations and included cotton, sugar, tobacco, molasses and rum.

Apparently Sam Bellamy wasn't hip to all that.

I took another sip of wine, thought about calling Ali, and didn't. His voicemail—and it wasn't even *his* voice on the mail, it was a special number I could call for someone, not him, to listen to, to pass on any important messages—already had enough of my voice on it. Instead I pressed my smartphone icon for Mirela. "What do you know about the Whydah?" I asked.

"Yes, thank you, sunshine, this is a good time to call," she said coolly. "You mean the pirate ship?" You'll never catch Mirela out, especially when it comes to Cape Cod lore. Maybe it's because she's smart. Maybe it's because people from other countries know more about our history than we do.

"Well, yeah, that one. How many Whydahs do you know about?" I asked crossly.

"You are still in a mood," she informed me again. "Are you asking about this ship to distract you from Ali, or from your mother?"

"Maybe a little of each," I said cautiously. "Humor me."

A sigh. "All right, then, wait a moment." She was lighting a cigarette; I could hear the first long inhale; she started speaking on the exhale. "It was a brand-new ship," she said. "It was coming back from Jamaica when the pirates saw it." She laughed. "They chased it all around the Caribbean for three days before capturing it."

I'd never heard that, nor had it been in my brief Internet reading; Mirela knows things no one else knows. I had an instant image of the two ships dashing around on a game board. "Wow," I said.

"Wow is a silly thing to say, sunshine."

Mirela can be obscenely tedious when she chooses. I took another swallow of wine. "Okay. Scratch that. What else do you know?"

"I know he was a *babe*," she said. "Everyone else wore silly powdered wigs, but not him. He had a wonderful mass of black hair he tied with a ribbon. He put ribbons around his weapons, too. That's how they decided it was his bones they found on the Whydah recently—that ribbon around the gun." She paused. "*I'd* have dated him," she said judiciously.

Who wouldn't? "Did anybody?" I asked.

"Some woman on the Cape," she said, dismissive. "That is who he was coming to see, on his way up to Maine. She ended up becoming crazy or something. I have forgotten exactly what happened to her."

That sounded interesting, though not particularly relevant. "What do you know about the Mignonette?" I asked instead.

"The whom?"

"Mignonette. Another slave-ship, a French one. A sloop, whatever that is. It was part of Bellamy's fleet. Apparently it went down in the same storm as the flagship."

Another inhale-exhale on the cigarette. "No. I never heard of it. Is that all, sunshine?"

"What, am I keeping you from something? You have a hot date?" I didn't want to hang up and start thinking about Things I Shouldn't Think About.

"With Netflix," she said.

Which will, sadly, beat me out every time.

5

Guy Husband was prompt. I was just stretching in bed, luxuriating in the fact that my apartment actually had heat, when my phone rang. I found it caught in the covers. "Sydney Riley."

"Guy Husband here," he said crisply. "If it's convenient, I can take you to Orleans now."

"Orleans?"

"Car rental," he said. "Your own car has been towed and is being serviced, but I want to make sure you have transport in the meantime."

I actually can go for days, weeks even, without using the Little Green Car—that may be part of the reason it's lasted so long—since Provincetown's small enough to walk or cycle pretty much anywhere; but we were in the cold season and he was right, I didn't really want to be walking anywhere. "Give me fifteen minutes?"

"I'll see you then," he said, and disconnected.

I scrambled out of bed, to Ibsen's delight: Sydney upright means Sydney about to feed him. "Not now, kiddo," I muttered as I quickly assembled jeans, sweaters, and long underwear. Fifteen minutes might not sound to anyone else like time enough for coffee, but I won't make it out the door without caffeine, so I threw the kettle on when it boiled I poured hot water into the French press while I was still pulling on my furry boots.

Guy Husband was, of course, early.

I hopped up into the SUV next to him and managed not to thank him again for going to all this trouble, since he was actually the cause of the trouble. I snuggled down into the heated seat (who doesn't love heated seats?) and reviewed my questions. It's a good half-hour's drive to Orleans, and I wanted to know more about what he was doing. "You said there were rumors around about the Mignonette," I said.

"Did I?" His voice was bland. "Your seatbelt, please, Ms. Riley."

"For heaven's sake." I fumbled and clicked the belt into place. "You hit my car, you get to call me Sydney. And you said there were rumors."

"You do come right to the point," he complained. "I'm feeling quite fine this morning, thank you for asking."

"The Mignonette," I said, not to be deterred. "Rumors."

He sighed. "Everyone knew something had sunk," he said, pulling out onto Bradford and heading for Shank Painter Road. The scene of the crime, as it were, since we were about the pass the Stop & Shop. "The rest of the fleet made it to Maine, minus the two ships, the Whydah and the Mignonette. But in the meantime… well, let's be clear, after every storm, what do people do? Head out to the beach to see what the storm tide brought in, right? That's what happens now. It wasn't any different then."

It was pretty much what John did, for sure. Tidewrack with a twist. I didn't say anything.

"In those days, more so than now for obvious reasons, it really paid to watch the shoreline," Guy said. "Back before the canal was built, there were some significant shipwrecks along this coast. I've forgotten how many, exactly—"

"I know all about the canal," I interrupted. I didn't need him lecturing me on Cape Cod, just on the damned pirate ship. "I *do* live here."

He glanced at me, then back at the road. "Very well. Bellamy's fleet was carrying treasure from fifty-three other ships in the Caribbean that they'd boarded or captured," he said. "It's probable no one knew they were out there, there's no reason why they should. That was probably true of all the shipwrecks; people didn't know anything until cargo and timber started washing up on shore. But then? People flocked to the beaches, especially as soon as anything of value showed up."

"Like what?"

He shrugged. "Like anything. Coins. Weapons. Jewels." He glanced at me. "Timber; that's how they built a lot of the houses, with materials from shipwrecks." Take that, Cape Cod Girl, his tone seemed to say. "But of course especially anything shiny. The governor—he was a colonial governor then, this was pre-American Revolution, you still were one of ours—sent someone down posthaste to claim anything else for the crown. And *that* fellow reported that more than two hundred men from as far as twenty miles away were busily appropriating whatever they could. They didn't name the ship; they didn't know it was Bellamy and his merry men; they just knew it was pirate loot, and everyone wanted in on it."

We turned right onto Route Six. "Nice people," I commented. "Not checking to see if anyone survived or anything helpful like that."

An amused glance. "Human nature," said Guy. "Self-enrichment before all else. But besides that, there were bodies, don't think for a moment there weren't. You seem to know your Whydah history, so you know there were only two survivors. The rest of the bodies—minus Bellamy and a few others—washed ashore and got dumped in a mass grave."

"That's the Whydah," I pointed out. "What about yours?"

His mouth curved into a smile. "Thank you for the ownership," he said. "I expect some of the supposed Whydah bodies were from the Mignonette. And it didn't happen all at once, either. Any others washing ashore—well, it's not like these two were the only shipwrecks from that storm. And a storm wasn't even necessary; there was a wreck every couple of weeks, I expect."

"So how did people know it was the Mignonette?"

"I'm not saying they did. It's not as if Captain Bellamy broadcast his intentions to anyone. I don't expect that at the time, to the people scavenging, it made much difference at all what any ship's name was. Soon thereafter, of course, that changed. There were rumors there was more than one pirate sinking—the artifacts were washing up in fairly disparate places, the Mignonette clearly made it considerably closer in to the bay than did the Whydah before she went down—but that's all. The only way to get pirate treasure, back then, was to sit and wait for wind and tide to bring it to you."

"Unlike now."

"Unlike now," he agreed.

"So how do you do it now?" The great thing about the Cape in the off-season is that Route Six goes back to being a highway instead of a parking lot, but we were still only in Wellfleet and I wanted to keep the conversation going.

"Sorry?"

"How do you do it now? How do you find the wreck? How do you identify it?"

He sighed. "Do you really want a lesson in marine salvage and underwater archaeology?"

"Just the high points will do," I assured him.

"One narrows it down to a suspected site," he said. "Through research, through discovered artifacts, a number of things go into it. Then one tows a proton precision magnetometer across the suspected wreck site. If it finds the presence of iron and steel, the magnetometer records a hit. At that point one can narrow down the exact position, how it is lying on the ocean bed, details such as those. By that time one is generally clear about what ship it is, of course, but finding artifacts on board with the name is naturally the preferred route."

"Naturally," I said blandly.

"It's how Whittier identified the Whydah for certain," he said. "Found the ship's bell with the name inscribed on it."

"I've seen it," I said. And I had; it's at the main Whydah museum in South Yarmouth, suspended in yellowish murky water, but you can read the inscription. Apparently stuff deteriorates when it's left in the air after being left in the sea. "Nice to have something so clear to prove you're right."

That earned me a glance. "And one isn't always right," he said. "Even the professionals; we're not always right." He was smiling at something.

"Come on," I said. "Tell me. What's so funny?"

"Robert Whittier," he said. "One could call us competitors, of course, and while one doesn't wish ill on one's fellow professional…" His voice trailed off, suggestive.

"Okay," I said. "Out with it."

"Nothing that won't get me sued," Guy said, shaking his head. Maddeningly. He must have known where my loyalties would lie

Like I said, we on the Cape feel rather possessive about the Whydah, and by association about Robert Whittier. I was willing to cut him a little slack. "So if you can't dive in November, why are you here now?" I asked bluntly, changing the subject so Guy would stop gloating. Okay, so he's not exactly Saint Robert of the Atlantic, but still…

I'd been pretty obvious; that earned me a quick glance, but he went with it. "Research," he said briefly. "I'm here to do research. And now, tell me, Ms. Riley, about what *you* do in Provincetown."

Talk about changing the subject, and not caring about subtlety. "I'm wedding and events coordinator at the Race Point Inn, the place you're apparently calling home while you're here," I said after a moment. "And I'm working some hours at an art gallery this winter."

"That's very concise."

"I'm not all that interesting," I said. "Come on, think about it! *You* blow into town ready to raise a pirate ship, and *I* help people get married. Not much comparison." I made my voice light; while it was true that I'm not changing history, I also really love my job and what I do in life and where I do it. I get to be with people on the best day of their lives; there's not much better than that. I become a part of their story forever.

I might not be a pirate-hunter; but I have no complaints.

Except, perhaps, when it came to my mother. Damn it, was there any way to *not* be thinking about her? "Here," I said. "You go three-quarters of the way around the rotary."

"The what?" He sounded startled; he hadn't been in the States long enough.

"The roundabout," I said helpfully. "That way."

If *pirate treasure* can't distract me from thoughts of my mother, then there's pretty much no hope at all.

***

I got the rental. I returned to P'town. Guy promised to keep me up to date with the progress on the Little Green Car, which I was happy to leave in his hands.

I went back home and made my bed, fed Ibsen, drank two more coffees, and contemplated the rest of my day. I still needed groceries. The gallery owner was expecting me to open at some point. Glenn wanted me to come over and meet about the wedding couple and some other unspecified thing.

I was also dying to tell someone about my adventures in pirate lore, but couldn't think of anyone who would be sufficiently impressed. I tried it out on Ibsen, who actually yawned in my face before settling into his current favorite place on the back of the sofa. So much for family support.

Oops. *Not* going to think about family. My mother was hovering in the back of my brain, but my heart was aching—or so I imagined, it could have been indigestion—wondering about Ali. And, yeah, it was time I accepted that he was family now. What was he doing right now? Who was he pretending to be? Why couldn't he get away long enough to touch base with me?

I finally headed over to the inn, where it was clearly on the cusp of all the festivities—the lighting of the Pilgrim Monument, the lighting of the lobster pot tree, the start of Holly Folly itself—and the place was looking like an updated version of Currier and Ives. All very Pottery Barn, of course; Mike, the inn's manager, is nothing if not devoted to The Gay Man's Style Guide. He could have been one of the Fab Five if he'd been a little younger, a little more famous, and a little more handsome; otherwise, he had it locked.

Everything that could glitter, glittered. Everything that could be polished shone. There wasn't an inch of space that wasn't occupied.

"What do you think?" Mike had come up behind me in the foyer, where a twelve-foot Christmas tree was currently being decorated by a couple of his minions; he was clearly delighted with his tinsel and garlands and lights.

"It's very enthusiastic," I said.

"Yeah, it is, isn't it?" He was smiling, the wonder of a child in his eyes, and I had to smile, too. So we don't have the same taste; that isn't everything. Besides, who was I to talk? I didn't even have the smallest holiday decoration yet in my little apartment, which looked like a back alley after the Broadway lights of the Race Point Inn. A neglected back alley.

I have a very special place in my heart for Mike. Even if he weren't a good guy—and he most definitely is—he also saved my life, once, fishing me out of the harbor during one rather memorable October when someone was trying very hard to kill me. You don't forget the little things like that.

"Sydney! That you?" It was Glenn, bellowing from Mike's office behind the front desk.

Mike and I exchanged eyerolls. "Coming, dear!" I called out, and added to Mike, "Gotta work a little on his Christmas spirit."

"You're telling me." He wandered back into the foyer to watch his myrmidons decorating the tree, and I headed into the office to see Glenn. "You rang?" I inquired from the doorway.

"What do you think," Glenn said, not raising his eyes from whatever papers he was frowning at on Mike's desk, "about doing something special here after the Lobster Pot Tree lighting? Some kind of reception?"

I slid into the chair in front of the desk. "I think you've left it a little late, if you're talking about this year," I said frankly.

"Yeah, I thought so, too. Thought I'd run it by you."

Glenn's relatively new to innkeeping and all the planning that's involved in running a pretty large operation like Race Point. It's definitely a steep learning curve. He inherited the inn from his partner, Barry, who was murdered—right here at the inn, actually—a few years ago, and he still really didn't have the knack.

Still, the timing seemed a little glaringly obvious. Holly Folly was going to be on us before any of us realized, and things just seemed to accelerate after that.

"We can plan to do something next year," I suggested. "What are you thinking, something intimate, or just throw open the doors to everyone?" We have enough space; the Race Point includes a full-service elegant rated restaurant, along with a separate dining-room and several bars. If anyone can pull it off, we can.

Glenn shrugged. "Whatever. That's not really what I wanted to talk about." He finally looked up from his papers and sighed heavily.

"I might as well just say it. Thing is, Sydney, I've had an offer on the inn."

I stared at him stupidly. Of all the things he might have brought up… I hadn't seen this one coming. "To *buy* it? An offer from whom?" I was instantly and completely against it, no matter what exactly "it" transpired to be. I like the people I work with. I like the way the inn is run. Glenn was settling in, Mike is a love, and even Adrienne, our diva chef, isn't someone I'd want to do without, though I'd never admit as much to her.

"Hotel chain." He was watching me. "What are your thoughts?"

"A *chain*?" I squeaked. It would be one thing to sell to someone who would run the inn the way Barry had envisioned it; something altogether else to make it like every other American-based hotel around the world. "But this is *P'town*!" We're very anti-chain anything in this town; Stop & Shop was grandfathered in (it had previously been a Grand Union, and before that an A&P), and CVS had to jump through hoops to get its store on Bradford Street—and there was still a lot of hostility toward it.

He looked back down at the papers, possibly so he wouldn't see my outrage. I couldn't read them from where I was sitting. "It's a generous offer," he said, slowly. "I haven't had the lawyers look at it yet, but the numbers seem to make sense." He paused, feeling my negativity in the air, hanging thick as smoke. "This isn't completely out of the blue. You know I never planned on being an innkeeper, Sydney."

"Would Barry have sold out?" The words were out of my mouth before I could stop them.

"It's not Barry's inn anymore," Glenn said sharply, more sharply than I'd ever heard him speak.

I wasn't about to be deterred. "No," I agreed. "It's not Barry's, it's yours, and it should *stay* yours."

"That's not up to you to decide." He was back to looking at the paperwork. He couldn't possibly be reading anything. "I have to think about the future. My future. I have to build something for myself. Maybe build something that's not rooted in the past." He rubbed his forehead; he suddenly looked about seventy. "Maybe I'm just tired, Sydney, I don't know. But right now it's sounding pretty good."

I took a quick breath, even leaned forward in my chair. "If you're tired of it, that's fine, Glenn, you don't have to be here, just don't give up on us altogether! We're a great team. Adrienne's famous, people come to stay here just for her, just to eat her cuisine. Mike runs the place beautifully, he's a magician, you know that. Give him more responsibility—hell, give *me* more responsibility if you want, but don't make us part of Best Western or Hilton or Choice or any of them…" My voice trailed off; I was suddenly dangerously close to tears.

Glenn was watching me. "All right," he said abruptly. "Don't go all soft on me. I knew that's what you'd say, anyway."

"Then why d'you make me say it?" The tears were still there. Tears for the inn, for my level of comfort working there, for Barry himself, probably. I was not going to cry in front of Glenn. I was *not*.

"I told you because you have a right to know what's going on," he said. "You have a right to know it's a possibility I'm considering. What I'm thinking about. Just *thinking*, Sydney, so don't take this anywhere it doesn't have to go. I haven't made a decision one way or the other. And even if I did, there's no guarantee the town would go for it."

Except that if it didn't go through, the possibility had become real. The next offer might be easier to accept—and push through the town's boards.

I stood up. "Is that all?" I probably sounded like a sullen adolescent. *Breathe, Riley*, I told myself. *Just breathe*. Glenn was being perfectly fair—I know enough other business owners in town, people who wouldn't breathe a word of a sale to their employees until it was a total fait accompli—and I didn't need to give him a hard time about it. And yet there I was.

Sometimes I don't even like myself very much.

He flapped a hand, tiredly, not willing to argue any more, not even looking at me, and I turned and escaped. Mike wasn't anywhere to be found, naturally, so I couldn't grab him and find out what he knew about the offer. *No crying.* Instead I tucked myself into the alcove behind registration that's euphemistically known as my office—it's a desk, a telephone, and a big calendar—and called the couple who wanted to get married. Left voicemail. Thought about what to do next. Stared at the wall for way too long.

The Race Point Inn was my life, in a whole lot of ways big and small that didn't bear thinking about—or considering losing. I wasn't like a lot of the other washashores; I hadn't come here for vacation one sunny summer, fallen in love with the town, and spent the next five years figuring out a way to move and live and work here. I hadn't started out looking for a new home, or new employment; I hadn't started out looking to become a wedding organizer. All of it had happened accidentally, and it had all happened because of Barry.

I'd chanced upon Provincetown completely haphazardly one winter. I was living in Boston and trying to figure out how to get out of a dying relationship, and finally I put together all my vacation and personal days from my job in one of the downtown PR firms and decided to send a week or so on the Cape (chosen totally at random, by the way) thinking about things. I'd found a cheap rental on Commercial Street—winter's the only time you can put the words cheap, rental, and Commercial Street next to each other in a sentence—and one frigid day had stopped at the Race Point Inn because it was one of the few places open for coffee.

Barry had been sitting in the lounge drinking hot chocolate and reading the New York Times, wearing a big intensely ugly sweater that said "Hug a Bear Today" in bright red letters. I sat in a chair near his, wrapped my hands around my steaming coffee, and asked, "What's a bear?"

He looked up at me, his eyes twinkling. By the time I left, I had a job offer.

I'd quit my Boston job, officially making the move to P'town permanent. I'd argued with my ex over custody of Ibsen (I won, though some days I wonder if he hadn't won that round), moved into a far smaller and more affordable apartment that Barry found for me, and learned how to organize weddings. I became close to Barry's partner Glenn, who only lived in town part-time, and to Mike and—okay, not to Adrienne the diva chef, but the point still remains. The Race Point Inn had become, in many of the most important ways, my home.

And the truth was I loved my work there. Yeah, it had its moments, but P'town doesn't really get much in the way of pushy mothers and crazed bridezillas, and honestly, you're always dealing with happy people, how cool is that?

I worked with people who genuinely cared about the town and what they were doing in it; I met guests from all over the world, learned customs and snippets of languages; I'd even met my boyfriend, Ali, through doing weddings at the inn, back when he was still on the bad-guy side of ICE enforcement. Like any job, it was everything from mildly exasperating to tear-your-hair-out crazy-making... and it was also filled with moments of sacred beauty and total euphoria. I couldn't imagine doing anything else.

And then Barry, my bear of a boss, had been killed.

Barry was the first major loss in my life, which says something, doesn't it, that I've managed to get through thirty-five-plus years without anyone close to me dying. Don't get me started on my mother; I don't actually wish her dead, just wish she'd go far, far away. Someone (or perhaps it was just a fortune cookie) said that when you lose someone, it's to make space in your life for someone else; and my only consolation, in those horrible weeks and months after Barry's murder, was that I'd met Ali. We'd had a rocky start, but he won me over and now... No; I wasn't going *there*.

I'd found it hard enough to imagine the Race Point Inn without Barry. Imagining it without his longtime partner—who somehow kept, for me at least, the *essence* of Barry around—was unthinkable.

It might not happen, I told myself fiercely. Glenn was just floating the idea. He was thinking about it; that was all. Of course he had a right to consider it; you'd be crazy not to, in his place. It was his life and his future, and he was the one who had been Barry's forever-love, not me. I was probably working myself up over nothing at all. Glenn had been kind enough to share his thoughts with me, and that was as far as it went. There was absolutely no reason to freak out over something that hadn't yet happened and that might never happen.

On the other hand, that's never stopped me in the past, and it wasn't about to stop me now.

6

Like most of Provincetown's year-round residents, I really pinch my pennies in the winter.

I don't draw a full-time salary from the inn because of the irregularity of my work, so I save as much of it as I can for the off-season. I'd been lucky, this winter, to find a few hours at the gallery, though that too would change in January when it closed for the requisite winter three months when the town is in a deep freeze and the wind screams down Commercial Street and hanging signs creak and scare the hell out of you. No one's shopping, much less looking at art. Most places can't keep the electricity on for the amount of sales they make in the deepest part of the off-season.

All that is to say this: eating out isn't on my winter agenda. But if any day called for an exception to that rule, today was that day. What I really, really wanted was to be someplace warm where there were other people and a glass of wine.

What that meant was Napi's.

Once upon a time, Napi van Dereck stood with other kids at the end of the pier and watched the ferries come in, back in the days when the ferries were elegant affairs with orchestras and gourmet meals and people dressed for the occasion. They'd come off the boat and throw coins into the harbor for the kids to dive for, and Napi remembers those days well. He grew up here and eventually owned an antiques shop with his wife, Helen; when they opened a restaurant they just transferred all the antiques into it, so it's filled with a variety of curiosities, a substantial and actually quite important art collection, and stained glass behind the bar, the whole rounded out by fairy lights all over the place put up one Christmas for part of a town-wide competition that just stayed on after that.

Now his was one of the few places in town open year-round, even offering lunch in the off-season, and, while it's not on the menu, if you ask very, very nicely, they'll give you a gypsy lunch of soup, a slice of bread, and a helping of salad.

I sat at the bar and got a glass of red Zinfandel, quickly, before I had time to think any more about the inn, and took a hefty swallow before looking around.

"Hi, Sydney," said the man sitting at the end of the bar, one seat away from me, looking up politely from his book and waiting for me to notice him. "It's funny; I was just thinking about you," he said.

I put down my glass; I probably shouldn't actually down it all at once, anyway. "Hi, James," I said. James Harrison, local historian, chair of the cemetery committee, and sometime gallery owner. Fortunately, not the gallery where I was working, or he might have had something to say about my midday glass of wine.

It seemed there was always someone occupying that seat at Napi's: for decades it had been Richard Olson, who'd only recently died, and was a human walking history of Provincetown, a living monument, whose absence was still felt and remarked upon with some frequency, joining the pantheon of P'town's illustrious dead. James drinks a little less than Richard, but seems to have really stepped up to the plate in carrying the torch otherwise.

Dan my favorite bartender came over and I ordered my lunch and started sipping the wine in a more ladylike fashion. James marked the page in his book with some deliberation and turned to me. "I saw your friend Mirela this morning," he remarked.

"I'm surprised she was out of her studio," I said. "She's going crazy, getting ready for Holly Folly."

"Ah, yes. Holly Folly. She does well then, doesn't she? No one's Holly Folly is complete without one of Mirela's paintings. Pretty soon none of us will be able to afford her."

"I've never been able to afford her." I said it with a wry smile. But he made a point: every year, it seemed, Mirela collected more devoted followers who seemed willing to pay anything to get one of her pieces for their home in New York City or San Francisco or London. I was beyond proud to be her friend.

James finished whatever was on his plate and pushed it away. "All set, Dan, thanks," he said, then turned back to me. "I'm glad I ran into you, actually," he said. "As I said, I was thinking of you just this morning. As our resident solver of mysteries, that is."

"I'm hardly that," I said; but even I had to admit there was some truth to the remark. For reasons beyond my understanding, I seem to have been at the center of more than a few devious goings-on in town, starting with Barry's murder, continuing with that unwanted dip in the harbor during a far-too-memorable Fantasia Fair, and moving into a Portuguese Festival I wasn't forgetting anytime soon. Not to mention Carnival. I didn't even want to *think* about last Carnival. I wondered briefly if I should be taking this all more personally than I'd been doing.

"Indeed you are. Scott Coffey says you're Provincetown's answer to Jessica Fletcher," he said.

"I don't write," I said automatically. I was too young to have ever watched *Murder, She*

Wrote on television, but it sure cast a long cultural shadow. And Scott Coffey—who owns Coffey Men on Commercial Street down near the Boatslip and makes eccentric and beautiful things for men to wear—was probably just being nice; that's the kind of guy he is. I should remember to thank him for noticing.

"In any case," said James, hauling us back to the subject, "I actually have a little mystery myself on my hands, and while—of course, don't worry, it's all official, I've taken it to the harbormaster's office—I thought you might want to have a go at solving it yourself."

Harbormaster? Oh, hell. That could only mean one thing. He was talking about the Mignonette. This shipwreck had to be the worst-kept secret ever. And no, I was not going to discuss pirate treasure more than once in one day. No, no, no. It was getting to be just a little too surreal. "James—" I began, put he was already pulling out his smartphone and scrolling through screen after screen. "Here we go. Found it yesterday," he said, and held the phone out to me.

I took it with some resistance. "What is it?" I asked reluctantly.

"What do you think it is?"

I finally looked down at the phone and frowned at the image. What I was seeing was essentially a piece of wood, a plank, taken from different angles and at different levels of magnification. It was sitting on sand and there was some dried seaweed caught on one corner. I glanced up at James but he was watching me intently, waiting.

I sighed and looked back at the photo. Words on the plank, but dimmed, no doubt by the effect of being in the water. I zoomed in and stared and then looked up at James again. "You're kidding," I said.

He shook his head. "No. You see what it is."

I looked down again at the phone in my hand. Once you saw it, it couldn't be anything else: the name of the vessel the plank had come from. The paint had flaked but the letters had been carved in. And they were just about legible. "The Bessie G," I said.

James nodded. "The Bessie G," he confirmed.

I handed him his phone and leaned against the back of my barstool, letting my breath out in one long exhalation. "Wow," I said at last, not thinking about how Mirela would scold my vocabulary. "Holy shit. They never left, after all."

He was looking smug as he flipped through the photos again. As well he might. The Bessie G is our own local unsolved mystery. Well one of them; there's still the dismembered woman's body found out in the dunes in the 1960s, and who knew if that one would ever be solved.

This was more recent; it happened about a year before I moved to P'town, but it was already well embedded in local lore, especially as it ended with a poignant and disturbing question mark.

The Bessie G was a fishing boat, rigged for scalloping, belonging to a local family named—what was it? I dredged the recesses of my memory. His first name was Tony… Correia, that was it. Tony Correia. One morning someone walking their dog under the pilings of a wrecked pier out in the East End, of all places, found Tony's body, propped up against the piling—with a bullet in his head. When the police went to deliver the news to his family, they found his wife, their two daughters, and the boat itself missing altogether, and though it's hard to believe that in the twenty-first century a fishing boat (or anything, for that matter) can just disappear into thin air, that was apparently what happened. No one ever heard from the Bessie G or any of the family again.

Naturally, speculation ran rampant. The wife and daughters had killed Tony and then taken off in the boat. This was quickly discounted: the family didn't own a gun, the wife had never indicated any discontent with her life, and then of course there was still that whole disappearing-into-thin-air thing.

A couple of our more eccentric residents (and Provincetown has a plethora from which to choose) advanced the possibility of a Bermuda Triangle-like effect in Cape Cod Bay; *that* one kept us entertained for a while. Everyone had some opinion about what happened.

People talked about drug-smuggling and old feuds; about love affairs and business deals gone bad; about random violence and revenge and a whole lot of other motives I couldn't begin to remember; but at the end of the day it still remained a mystery. The Bessie G had disappeared, Tony Correia had been shot, and no one, as they say, knew nothing.

"The Bessie G," I said, now, to James. "So it did sink, after all."

"Seems so," he said, nodding.

Dan came over with my lunch. The soup smelled good. "There you go," he said, putting it down and then glancing at James. "He show you his pictures?"

I nodded. "Can you believe it?"

"I always thought she'd run off," Dan said. "Seriously, it seemed the most logical option."

"She didn't shoot him," I pointed out.

"We don't know that," he said, and went to fill another order. I buttered my bread and looked at James. "What are you going to do about it?"

"Huh?" He looked startled. "What do you want me to do? I'm not doing anything. I've done what I can. I turned it over to Roger. He'll do whatever's supposed to be done. I don't even know what that is."

Roger is the harbormaster in Provincetown, and to mix clichés, he runs a very tight ship out there on the pier. He's weathered a lot of storms, and not just of the meteorological kind.

He'd probably taken the disappearance of the Bessie G personally; it had happened on his watch, so to speak.

I knew from my friend Julie Agassi, who's a detective with the Provincetown police, that *they* had taken the bullet in Tony's head pretty personally, too.

James was watching me. "So when I saw you, I thought, something for you to do, maybe," he said.

I spooned soup into my mouth and thought about it for a moment. "What do you mean?"

He smiled. "Well, come on. It's the off-season, so you have some time on your hands right now, don't you? No weddings? What else do you have to do, besides solve a mystery?"

Put like that, it sounded one hell of a lot better than worrying about my boyfriend being undercover with—and in danger from—human traffickers in California, the inn and my livelihood being threatened, or my mother's imminent arrival. Actually, a mystery suited me to a T.

The problem, of course, is that I'm not *really* a detective. Things seem to happen to people around me and I try and figure things out, but most of the time I stumble around from one clue to the next and occasionally get lucky. As a detective, I behave as though I were in a pinball machine, bouncing around to whatever is shiny in my path.

Besides, real detectives had tried to solve this one, and failed. The state police had been in. The district attorney had been involved. The gun that shot Tony Correia had never been found. "There's not much to go on," I said to James.

"There's more than there was yesterday," he said cheerfully. "Eat your soup before it gets cold, Sydney."

I ate my soup.

***

I opened the gallery, plugged in the electric heater, and sat trying to thaw out for three hours, during which no one came in, no one called, and pretty much nothing happened.

I did spend some time thinking about the Bessie G and didn't get any farther than anyone else had done in the past eight years. Sure, Tony's wife could have taken it out. But where? And why? And who just drops their lives and disappears like that? Criminals, the Mafia—I didn't know. Certainly not a Portuguese fishing family from Provincetown. Besides, even if something had happened on the boat, how had Tony ended up on land, in the East End, and fatally shot? One went round and round and round with thoughts like that.

About half an hour into the afternoon I called Mirela. "When did you come to town?" I asked. "I mean, when did you move here for good?"

"Years ago, sunshine," she said. "I do not remember exactly. Why? Who keeps count?"

It didn't matter. "Do you remember the murder of that guy they found under the pier in the East End? The fisherman?"

"Of course I do, sunshine. I lived right over one of the shops then—I watched it all, from my back window, the police coming and going, and they Scotch-taped off the area—is that how you say it?—and I had to go around the tape to get in and out of my apartment for many days. I even saw the van taking him away. The poor man."

"Do you know who shot him?"

"What do I look like to you, sunshine, part of the Bulgarian mafia? How am I supposed to know?"

I was startled. "There's a Bulgarian mafia?" I'm easily sidetracked.

"There is a mafia everywhere, sunshine. And the truth is people get shot everywhere."

"Not in Provincetown, they don't." Well, unless *I'm* around, of course; my presence does seem to help rack up the bodies. I've celebrated nearly every theme week by finding one, or dealing with one, or something. Still, I couldn't actually take credit—or blame, depending on how you looked at it—for Tony Correia; he'd been killed before I even spent my first full winter here.

Mirela sighed. "Well, I do not know who killed that fisherman, me. It is not something I have thought much about."

"No," I acknowledged. "One doesn't." I wondered if he had any family left. *They* probably thought about it. A lot.

She was tapping something; it sounded unnaturally loud in my ear. "So is it that you are bored, Sydney? Is it already too far into the off-season? Is this why you are talking about history like this?"

"Bored? How could I possibly be bored?" Sarcasm doesn't necessarily translate well through the phone, and certainly not into Bulgarian. "I had lunch at Napi's," I said.

There was a pause. "Well, then, that explains it."

Okay, so maybe sarcasm *does* work on the phone. I ignored it. "Yesterday James Harrison found part of the Bessie G washed up on the beach," I said.

A pause. "This is the fisherman's boat, this Bessie G? The one that disappeared after he was killed?" She didn't wait for my answer. "Of course it is, or else you would not have asked me if I remembered. How does James know it is the same boat?"

"The name's on it," I said. I walked over to the big plate-glass window at the front of the gallery to stare out at Commercial Street. For a moment I didn't recognize the car parked outside; my rental. "Did I tell you someone hit my car at the Stop & Shop?"

Another sigh. "Sunshine, you are having a busy time this week."

"You don't know the half of it," I said truthfully. Ali's absence was starting to hurt like a toothache, sharp and piercing and demanding, receding before coming back again stronger, a dark presence in the background of every thought, every conversation. I wouldn't have thought I'd miss him like this. I wouldn't have thought I'd miss anybody like this. "Anyway, I have a rental car now for a few days."

"It was bad, then?" Her voice sharpened. "You are all right, sunshine, yes?"

"I'm fine." And suddenly I didn't want to be having this conversation. I didn't want to be having any conversation, actually. "I have to go, Mirela."

There was a pause. "Do you want to come to dinner tonight and talk with me?"

Not particularly. "No, you have a lot to do, getting ready for your Holly Folly sales. Let's meet at the Lighting."

"That is not for three days," she said.

"I know," I said. "I'm fine, really I am."

"Okay." She didn't sound convinced. That was all right: neither was I. There were tears pressing up against my eyes. I wanted to hear Ali's voice and know he was all right. I wanted the Little Green Car back. I wanted to make sure I still had a job at the inn. I wanted to forget my mother was coming for Christmas. Most of all, I wanted to hear from Ali, to just hear his voice, to know he was all right, to know he'd be coming home soon. *Breathe, Riley: just breathe.* I was *not* going to cry.

"I'll call you tomorrow," I said, making a rash promise I might not keep if I felt the same way I did just then, and disconnected. Tried to breathe some more. Turned off the heat and the lights in the gallery, locked the point-of-sale tablet away, closed the gallery. Wondered how far I'd make it before I really did start crying. Wondered if I had anything in the apartment for dinner.

Wondered if Holly Folly was going to somehow blow up all around us.

7

Thea called when I was partway through some Stupid TV (how many British baking shows can you binge-watch? I was going for the record). Netflix was about all I felt reasonably able to tackle in my mental and emotional state. I hadn't heard anything from Ali. My mother, on the other hand, had left three voicemails, all of which I was ignoring; I almost didn't pick up the phone.

For Thea, however, I would. She'd just moved to town this past year and had been helpful during a small crisis we'd had (something we affectionately call Carnival), and that's *definitely* a story for another time. We'd gone out sailing a few times together after that, had the occasional cocktail at the Aqua Bar before the summer ended, and talked about everything under the sun. She was petite and African-American and extremely fierce.

"Mirela called me," Thea reported. "She's worried about you."

"So she said," I acknowledged. "What I didn't know was she was worried enough to go enlisting outside help. Are you on the cheer-Sydney-up-committee?"

Thea's used to my sarcasm. "A committee of one," she said, and laughed. "But it's my sworn duty. So, what do you say? Want to go to a movie?"

It was cold out. I was driving a rental car I didn't really know very well. "I don't think so, but thanks."

"You didn't even ask me what's playing."

"I don't even care what's playing." We have one movie theater in town, affiliated with the Provincetown International Film Society, that shows a lot of art films and stuff with subtitles. Not even in the same league as Stupid TV. At that moment, I probably couldn't think my way out of a box. An open one.

A sigh. "She's right. You *are* in a mood."

I relented. "Sorry. It's nice of you to care, Thea. I'm really grateful. Thanks for asking. I'm just exhausted, that's all. I'm really fine underneath it all There's just too much going on right now."

"Well, come with me to the Lighting, then," said Thea. "I can pick you up if you want. You shouldn't go alone."

"No one's alone at the Lighting," I pointed out. The whole town is there; it's even better than the Stop & Shop for catching up, albeit quite a lot colder.

"But we can go together," she said persuasively. "You can even come over to the house afterward." She paused. "I have a bottle of Châteauneuf-du-Pape," she added enticingly.

Thea does know my weak spots. "And you want me to help drink it? Wouldn't you rather just share it with Claudia?" Claudia was Thea's current girlfriend; she'd had a short and extremely disastrous marriage recently and wasn't in a hurry to try matrimony out again.

"There's enough in a bottle for three of us," Thea said. "Come on, say you will, it'll be fun."

"Okay." I may be feeling antisocial, but I'm not verifiably crazy. No one in their right mind turns down Châteauneuf-du-Pape. Besides, I did actually like Thea and Claudia, which was more than I could say for much of the world with the mood I was in.

"Good, then. I'll tell Claudia."

There was a pause. She was probably thinking about how to say good-bye. "Thea," I said finally, tentatively, "I know you're still kind of new to town. Did anyone—tell you about the Bessie G?"

"Of course," she said promptly. "It was a fishing boat. There's some kind of mystery around it, right? It disappeared one night, something like that?"

"That's the one." I hesitated. "Um... Thea... Do you have a minute? Something's going on... at least I think it might be... and maybe I'm just imagining things."

"Of course I have time," said Thea comfortably. I pictured her in the large gracious living-room of the large gracious house she and Claudia shared in the West End, velvet drapes drawn against the darkness, a fire crackling in the fireplace. "What's going on?"

"That's just it," I said uncomfortably. "I don't know if anything really is going on or not." I paused. "You know how in detective novels, someone, it's usually the cop, always says, I don't believe in coincidences?"

"Uh-huh."

"Okay, so maybe that's not what I'm trying to say, because I do actually believe in coincidences, otherwise there wouldn't be a word for it in our vocabulary, but anyway…" I took a deep breath and pulled myself together. *Breathe, Riley.* "So after the storm last Saturday, John Silva—you know John Silva, right?—he was checking out the beaches, like he does, and he found this coin. Old coin. He says it's off a pirate ship."

"The Whydah?" Thea may be new to the Cape, but she's been indoctrinated.

"Well, that's the thing, see. John says it's not in the right place for the Whydah, whatever that means, and anyway, there isn't any more loose change spilling out from the Whydah, Robert Whittier and his crew got it all, or are getting it all, or something. What's left is stuff that's stuck into other materials—I forget what that's called."

"Concretion," said Thea. She knows the most extraordinary things.

"Yeah, concretion. Anyway, all that means is this isn't from the Whydah. And John knew this guy—well, okay, believe it or not, that's really his name, actually, Guy Husband."

"You've got to be kidding!" She was laughing.

I shrugged; she couldn't see it. "Really," I said. "You couldn't make this shit up. So anyway, here's the thing, Guy Husband does what Robert Whittier does. Salvage and underwater exploration, old shipwrecks, and all that sort of thing."

"How does John know him?"

"Some story about working with him in Scotland or something, I can't remember," I said impatiently. "Anyway, that's not the point. The point is, as soon as John tells him—this is last Sunday or Monday—this guy, *Guy*, hops onto a private plane—a private plane, Thea, that impressed the hell out of John, not that I don't agree with him—and comes out to the Cape, even though he can't dive it this time of year. Says he's doing research. Says it's from the wreck of another ship that was part of Bellamy's fleet, a French ship called the Mignonette." I took another deep breath.; my words were coming out a little too fast. "So then, here's the coincidence part, finally: after that same storm last Saturday, Peter Harrison's walking his dog on the beach and he finds something washed up, too, and this one you're not going to believe: it's something off the Bessie G. The name's right on the damned thing."

I stopped. There was a moment of silence. I got up and poured myself a glass of water from the filtration pitcher on the counter. Finally Thea said, thoughtfully, "You know, Sydney, you're right."

"I am? What are you thinking?"

"What I'm thinking," she said, "is it's a co-incidence." She paused. "Listen, slow down a minute, think about it. What's so weird about two different artifacts washing up from the same storm? How can that be unusual? It happens all the time, stuff washes up, and if you'll think about it, last Saturday's was a doozy. Me and Claudia lost a whole bunch of shutters from the house, and there was a big tree came down right across from Relish." I felt her concern: Relish is a lovely seasonal breakfast-bakery-sandwich shop that's only yards from Thea's house. "And the power was out, remember? For almost five hours?"

"The power always goes out in a nor'easter," I said. I was disappointed in her reaction. What had I expected? A dramatic gasp or two? An offer to help me solve the mysteries?

"Yes, that's right, it always goes out, and especially when it's bad. You saw how much erosion was out at Herring Cove, it was in the *paper*, for heaven's sake. It's not unreasonable to think it loosened stuff from two wrecks." She paused. "Still, you have to wonder…"

"What?"

"Well," and she drew the word out, "it's probably just us assigning meaning to something that might not have any meaning at all, right? But you're right—you can't help but wonder about stuff coming ashore—no matter when it came ashore—from two separate wrecks that most people didn't even know were out there."

"No one even knew the Bessie G *was* a wreck," I said.

"Yeah," said Thea. "That's what I'm talking about. It does make you wonder." She paused. "Who's looking into it? Besides you, I mean."

"I'm not looking into anything," I said.

She laughed. "Of course you are. You're the only one in town who doesn't think of Sydney Riley as a detective."

"Amateur detective," I reminded her.

"Amateur, then. Just like—"

"Don't say it," I interrupted. "I'm not as old as Jessica Fletcher."

"You're not as *fictional* as Jessica Fletcher, either," she said. "But you have to admit you've got a reputation, Sydney."

"The point is, it's not even *one* investigation," I said. "James told the harbormaster and the police about the Bessie G. John told Guy Husband about the Mignonette. Except he didn't know it was the Mignonette; Guy's the one who knew that."

"So go to the Provincetown Police. Talk to your friend, Julie, is that her name? She's probably the one looking into it." Thea sighed. "After all these years, the Bessie G," she said reverently. "God, Sydney, I wonder if they're on it."

"The family," I said. It wasn't a question. A wife, two daughters.

"The family," she agreed. "Can they tell, after this much time?"

"I don't know." I poked Ibsen with my foot so he'd stop scratching himself. "But I know who I can ask."

***

I was oddly apprehensive about heading into the Race Point Inn the next morning. Nothing had happened overnight, I told myself; nothing had yet been decided. There wasn't going to be a big Four Seasons sign across the front of the building. But I felt something cold and heavy in the pit of my stomach as I went through the front door, resplendent in twinkling lights and fresh spruce garlands. *Breathe, Riley*, I reminded myself. *Deep breaths. Deep, deep breaths.*

Mike was sitting at my desk behind reception, looking over a checklist. "Please, just make yourself at home," I said, unwinding my scarf and shrugging out of my coat. It takes ten minutes to dress and undress in the winter, I swear it does. And Mike has his own office, he doesn't need my desk.

He glanced up. "Holly Folly," he said.

I rolled a client chair around and wedged myself into the alcove with him. I hadn't planned our Holly Folly presence—it's not exactly an event or activity—but Mike and Adrienne and I had spent a whole lot of time in October deciding what we would serve, what music we'd play, what gift cards we'd distribute, and what grade champagne we'd buy. "What's the problem?"

"No problem. Just being obsessive," he said.

That's fine; Mike's obsessiveness is one of the reasons the Race Point is consistently rated P'town's top inn. That rating meant a lot to him—well, to all of us, but to Mike in particular. I touched his arm. "What are you hearing about Glenn selling?" I asked, my voice low. The kid at the front desk didn't need to know about this.

Mike gave him a glance, anyway. "Offer's been made," he said shortly.

"I did gather that," I said tartly. "What's Glenn going to decide, do you think?"

He shrugged. "Can't read his mind," he said, then relented. "I don't know, but I'll tell you, I'd be surprised if he sold, once it comes down to it," he said.

I expelled a breath I hadn't realized I'd been holding. "Because of Barry?"

He shook his head. "I don't think so. Well, it started with being about Barry, maybe, but I think he likes the place now, I think he's settled into it. It's a lot of work, and he needs to delegate more, but I think he knows that." He glanced at me. "Don't look so scared, Sydney. An offer like this? It's kind of like someone asking you to marry them. You might end up saying no, but it's nice to be asked."

"Uh-huh." Most marriage proposals don't include multi-million-dollar enterprises, at least not the ones I'm familiar with, but the analogy worked. "Nice to know someone cares," I said, nodding.

He gave me a little half-smile and squeezed my arm. "We'll see," said Mike. "Cripes, what would he do, anyway, if he sold? Hang out in South Beach and drink margaritas all day? He wouldn't be able to go back to work, not with that kind of money in his pocket."

Right at that moment, hanging out in South Beach and drinking margaritas all day sounded pretty good to me. I shook the thought off and moved the conversation along. "You know that guy who's staying here, the one with the big SUV?"

He looked pained. "You just described half the guests."

I didn't know how to describe Guy Husband, but I was going to have to stop using "guy" as a common noun to do so. And he'd probably not written "famous underwater archaeologist and salvage specialist" on his registration card. "Tall, very blue eyes, hair graying, distinguished," I said helpfully. "English."

"Guy Husband," he said. "Why didn't you say so? What about him?"

"Is he in?"

The pained look was back. "Do you really think I keep tabs on everybody?" He sighed and raised his voice. "Chris!"

The kid at the front desk turned around. "Yeah?"

"Guy Husband. Did you see him go out this morning?"

"He's still at breakfast," Chris said.

Mike nodded at me. "Still at breakfast," he repeated. "Chris notices all the good-looking guys."

"Especially the ones with money," said Chris with a smile. "The single ones with money."

"Is he gay?" I asked. "The guest?"

Chris shrugged. "Don't get the vibe, but never say never," he said cheerfully.

I got up and wheeled my chair back where it belonged. "I'll put in a good word for you," I promised, and headed over to the dining-room, where the breakfast chef, Angus, was presiding over a buffet enhanced by Christmas candles, lights, and still more garlands. Not that Angus' buffets ever needed enhancing. There was music, too, piped in thoughtfully low, and it seemed to be classical-style renditions of holiday music. Always classy, the Race Point Inn.

I spotted Guy Husband right away. Sitting at a table by himself, a cup halfway to his mouth, frowning at a newspaper. The New York Times.

I'd frown at it, too, if I could afford to read it. I slid into the seat across from him and gestured toward his cup. "I thought all Englishmen drank tea," I said.

He glanced up. "We've adopted a number of American habits," he said. "Good morning, Ms. Riley."

"Sydney," I corrected automatically.

"Sydney, then. May I offer you some coffee?"

I shook my head. "I'm good, thanks."

He refolded the newspaper and put it down. "I'm afraid I don't have news of your car yet," he said.

"That's fine. The rental's great. That's not why I'm here," I said.

He raised his eyebrows. "Interested in more pirate stories?" he asked.

"In a manner of speaking." I took a breath. "Listen, I know you don't want to give away trade secrets, or anything like that, but—well, something else has come up. It might not be connected at all. But I thought you might be able to help."

"Of course," he said politely. "Anything I can do."

Another breath. "James—um, someone's found more wreckage. Same storm that brought you here, but a different boat."

"I see." He was managing not to correct my characterization of his discovery as a boat. I appreciated that.

I moistened my lips. "Um, so it's a different thing altogether. This is a fishing boat, it disappeared a few years ago—seven or eight. Its owner was shot, and the boat disappeared. And now part of it has washed up. Same storm as yours." I looked to see how he was reacting. "Coincidence, right?"

"Perhaps." He touched the linen napkin to his lips and pushed his chair slightly farther from the table—and me. I tried not to take it personally. "Tell me about this fishing-boat," he said. "The owner—was he shot on the boat?"

"No," I said, hoping I didn't look as startled as I felt. "No, of course not. He was shot here. Well, farther down toward the east end. There used to be tons more piers in town—oh, forty or fifty of them. They all get destroyed in storms. A couple of them didn't get completely demolished, you've probably seen them, just some pilings. It's all very picturesque; photographers are always out there trying to get them in the best light." Which there's not a dearth of here; it's one of the reasons Provincetown's the oldest art colony in North America. Everyone says it's the light. "He was shot down there, and either collapsed against the piling or whoever shot him propped him up there." I really should look up the old newspaper stories; the truth was I really didn't know any of the details.

"I see," Guy said again. "And his boat disappeared?"

I took a deep breath and let it out slowly. "Along with his wife and two daughters," I said.

Another eyebrow lift. "And the assumption was they killed him and sailed off into the sunset?"

I shrugged. "The assumption was everything from alien abduction to a drug deal to professional rivalry," I said. "In short, nothing. No one knew. And now this bit's come ashore—"

"What bit was that?"

"I don't know. A piece of wood."

"And yet you know it is from this missing fishing boat?"

I nodded. "The name was on it," I said, "Well, almost the whole name, the first letter was broken off a bit. But you could still read it. And I had a question about—"

He interrupted me, something I had a feeling he didn't do very often. "What is the name?"

"Excuse me?"

"The name," Guy said. "The name of the boat."

I stared at him. "You've probably never heard of it," I said, then, seeing him making a gesture of impatience, I added quickly, "The Bessie G."

It was impossible to tell from his expression how he was taking that in. And anyone can tell you, I've never been very good at reading people. But there was something there I didn't really trust.

I should listen to my gut more often.

8

He wasn't about to tell me what it was. He wasn't about to tell me anything, actually; Guy made a very hurried exit from the dining-room, and I never did get to ask him about whether or not the Correia family—were they on board—would be recognizable. Salvageable, in terms of bones and burials and funerals and so on. There was some family left in town, I thought; they'd want to know, surely.

Not my business. Roger the harbormaster was on top of it, certainly.

Guy's abrupt departure at the mention of the Bessie G meant something. I just hadn't a clue what that was.

He wasn't about to be trapped in a car with me again, either, to give me a chance to ask. Two days passed and there was a message on my voicemail: "Please leave the rental car in front of your house with the keys under the visor."

I called him back, of course. "Why am I leaving my keys under the visor?"

"Not *your* keys," Guy said, mock-patiently. "The keys to the Toyota. And remove anything of yours you might have left inside." He'd seen the Little Green Car; he knew what a tight ship I ran. I'm always promising myself to clean out the car. The problem is, when you live in a place as small as mine, there's always a little overflow.

All right: a lot of overflow. "And what happens then?" I asked.

"We'll leave your Honda there. Keys under the visor," he said.

"It's fixed?" I was squeaking with delight. Finished—and fast, for the Cape. You could tell it was the off-season. "But don't you want me to—"

He cut me off. "It's all taken care of," he said smoothly. "And, again, I apologize for any inconvenience I've caused."

Well. That was that. I felt curiously deflated, as though the issue of the car had set up a line of communication between us, established a casual intimacy that would disappear as soon as the reason for it did. The truth was, I *did* want to know more about the Mignonette, and I *did* want to know more about the Bessie G, and I was quite sure Guy Husband held the key to both.

And Guy Husband was making it clear he didn't want to talk about it. Any of it. "Okay," I said, dampening my enthusiasm. "Well, thanks.

Are you staying in town for the Lighting of the Monument? That's tomorrow night."

"Yes, I've heard about it," he said smoothly. "I expect to be here."

All right then. I took a deep breath. "Well, maybe I'll see you then," I said. "It's a really great event. It's usually dedicated to a group of people who need light in their lives for some reason—"

"Yes," he said, but now he was sounding amused. "So they told me at the inn."

I didn't just have my tourism spiel in high gear for the hell of it; I really did want to hear his plans. "And there's hot apple cider and cookies—"

"The ultimate inducement," said Guy. He was trying not to laugh. "Very well. I take it you are angling to go together?"

I hadn't been, exactly, but now that he mentioned it… "I didn't want to be too subtle," I said.

"I don't think that's much of a risk. What's the form? Does one walk up the hill?"

I shivered. "Too cold," I said. "We can park in the lot if we get there early, or across the street."

He sighed, giving in. "And the festivities begin at…..?"

I was ready. "Five o'clock," I said.

"Very well. I shall call for you at four-thirty. I have no idea why I'm doing this, mind you."

"The pleasure of my company?" I suggested.

"Something like that," he agreed, and disconnected.

I was trying to figure out which of the clothes I hadn't worn since last Christmas should really be packed up to the Methodist thrift shop when the phone rang again. I was wondering whether I'd ever wear plaid again and had my arms full of flannel, so I snatched it up and swiped before looking at the Caller ID. Bad mistake.

"Sydney! I've left you three messages!"

I took a deep breath. "I know, Ma. I've been busy."

"You know I've left you messages? They came through? So that means you listened but couldn't be bothered to return the call? This is how I brought you up?" She paused for a breath. "Besides, you've been busy doing *what*? I thought this was your off-season. God know, you talk enough about this season and that season, but it seems to me that someone could find five minutes to talk to their mother, no matter what the season."

If my mother ever has a conversation lasting five minutes the heavens will open and manna will rain down. In desperation, I played my trump card. "Ma, I was in a car accident."

She gasped. "Sydney! Sydney! Wait—I can be on my way, I just have to—"

Okay, that was just a *little* more reaction than I'd wanted. My mother's middle name is Excessive. "Ma, I'm fine. It's all good. I wasn't hurt. But I've had to deal with things—you know, getting the car fixed, renting another car, dealing with the insurance company." Okay, so none of that was true, but when it comes to my mother, you really have to haul out the major artillery.

"Have you seen a doctor? Sometimes you don't know you're hurt, but—"

"I wasn't *in* the car at the time," I said. "It got hit in the parking lot at the grocery store. It's all fine, really, it is."

"So if it's all fine, what are you doing, giving me a heart attack like that? You couldn't tell me right from the beginning that you're all right? Instead you let me think you're lying in a hospital somewhere. I think I'll sit down. I need to sit down. You are going to be the death of me."

This must be what they called mutually assured destruction, because I was pretty sure she was going to be the death of *me*. "Ma, you asked why I haven't talked to you in, what three days? I'm just telling you."

"Well, thank heavens you bothered to pick up the phone this time, or I'd have never known. Honestly, I don't know what goes through your head. *And* I don't know if you've looked at a calendar, and maybe you're comfortable waiting until the last minute, but your father and I like making plans, and it's already November."

"It was already November when you called me three days ago at six o'clock in the morning," I said.

"And I didn't know then that we'd be traveling, or I would have called you sooner!" she exclaimed triumphantly. My mother will twist logic to suit her need to score points.

I gave up. "So what do you need to know?"

"Well, just a few things," she said, the sarcasm coming through loud and clear. "We can start with the dates. Always start with the dates. If we're going to get tickets—"

"Wait," I said. "Tickets to what, exactly?" There's a symphony orchestra on Cape Cod, but my parents never showed any interest in classical music. No opera that I knew of.

"Well, to flights, of course," she said.

Flights? "You live in the next state up from me," I said. "Dad just got a new car last year." See, I do pay attention. Take that. "What are you talking about?"

"We're getting too old for the drive," she said and paused. I was clearly expected to add in a background of violins, or at least a protestation about their youthfulness. "We've looked it up, and we can fly Cape Air out of New Hampshire and arrive right there in Provincetown."

This was a nightmare waiting to happen. "Ma, that flight goes through Boston," I said. I have a lot of experience arranging flights; transportation is all part of the event-planning services from the Race Point Inn. "That means it's really two separate flights. You fly to Boston, you get out of the airplane, you wait for another airplane, you get on that one and it takes you to Provincetown."

"I don't see the problem," my mother said stiffly.

"It's going to be December," I said. "And Provincetown is a small, local airport. We don't have the kind of maintenance there is at Logan." Or in New Hampshire, for all I knew. I took a deep breath and tried to sound reasonable. "Flights don't land in P'town if there's no visibility. Flights don't land in P'town if the winds are too high." Either or both of which were quite probably what they'd encounter. Hell, it had already *snowed*, for heaven's sake, and we never get snow in November. And Cape Cod's winds are notorious.

What that meant was while my parents might get the flight out of New Hampshire, it was a crapshoot as to whether they'd get any farther. Well, Boston for sure: if they could take off—and that was still a strong *if*—then they'd land safely in Boston. There are only two flights in and out of Provincetown in the winter. So then there would be a hotel for the night, and my mother—here's a surprise—has strong opinions about airport hotels. Then the next day we'd have to see if the weather cleared.

Alternately, of course, I could drive to Boston and pick them up at Logan. Which would be a lot less comfortable in the Little Green Car than if they'd just drive themselves all the way in my father's top-of-the-line whatever it was he'd just bought.

"Stranded," I said to my mother. The word sounded scary enough. "You could end up *stranded*."

"Don't be melodramatic," she said, which was a little rich, coming from her. "I'm sure the airline knows what it's doing. Here's what I want to know. Can we reserve an aisle seat? You know how your father likes to stretch his legs."

"Ma," I said, "if you fly to P'town on Cape Air, every seat is an aisle seat. I don't think you understand. This is a very, very small airplane. You will feel every bit of turbulence." I wasn't actually fear-mongering, or at least not completely: I've been on small planes when it felt like we were on board an out-of-control elevator. I'm not crazy about the sensation. No one knows that about me. "There is no room at all for Dad's legs. It will be uncomfortable and even if you get the connection in Boston you'll be exhausted." I was substituting "exhausted" for "cranky," and who said I can't be nice?

She wasn't finished. "Exhausting? Really? Is that what you think? And you think asking your father to drive all that way *isn't* exhausting?"

My father used to do outside sales before he retired. He was in his car—and away from my mother and me, probably not coincidentally— for a good percentage of his career. He never found driving exhausting. He could drive to the Cape in his sleep.

But I was seeing a glimmer of light. "You're right," I said, inspired. "You're absolutely right. It's a rough flight and a rough drive and it's a difficult time of year, there could be a snow- storm." Well, maybe up where she lived. "Be- sides, everyone's traveling then. Let's postpone until the weather's better. Maybe you can come down in April or May."

She sniffed. "I think not. By then you'll be in your famous *season*"—I could imagine the air- quotes she put around the word—"and you won't have time for either of us. We'll just have to manage."

Oh, my God. I tried to count to ten. *Breathe, Riley. Just breathe.* "You know what?" I said. "Do what you want, Ma. Take the plane. Drive down. Take the bus. Whatever. You're going to do what you want anyway." There. I'd said it. I was rude to my mother. I was probably going to hell.

There was a pause. I waited for her to have hysterics, or told me about my attitude, or maybe even to smite me dead long-distance.

"There's a bus?" she asked.

***

We finally worked out a compromise. My mother's idea was they'd come for the Lighting of the Monument (in two days' time) and stay through Holly Folly and all the way to the day after Christmas, picking up a nice family Thanksgiving along the way. *My* idea was they'd never come as long as I was alive and well and living in P'town.

We settled on a plan that probably pleased neither of us: they would come sometime in the days before Christmas—no more than three of them—and leave before New Year's. *Well before* New Year's.

The plus side was they wouldn't be with me for Thanksgiving, because that would become far too political, and I could enjoy the various local traditions, including Holly Folly, without having to explain everything to my mother in excruciating detail. I couldn't see my mother making it through Holly Folly alive if she were here with me. I love it too much.

The downside was that I was going to have to make some kind of effort at decorating my apartment, as well as… well, I'd be spending Christmas with my mother. Enough said.

"I'll talk to your father about the airplane," she said, winding down. "We'll let you know. Can you get us discount tickets if we decide to fly?"

My parents might not be in the one-percent of Americans who control most of the wealth in this country but they're definitely in the top twenty percent. They have a Great Room, though I've never figured out exactly what's supposed to be so great about it. They lease a new car every other year. They use "summer" as a verb. Even if I could get them a discount on Cape Air—and I couldn't—there was no chance in hell. Maybe rich people get to be rich by being cheap. It wasn't the first time I'd had that thought.

"Ma," I said. "I have to go."

"Not so fast," she said. "I want to know who else will be there."

I sighed. "No," I said. "You don't want to know who else will be there. You want to know if Ali will be there."

She sniffed. "I would assume not," she said. "They don't celebrate Christmas, do they?"

I was feeling cranky enough to press the point. "Who's they, Ma?"

"You know exactly who I'm talking about, Sydney. Don't take that attitude with me. I swear I don't understand why you feel like you need to take that attitude with me. There are a lot of daughters who don't. Why—"

"Ma," I interrupted. "We've had this conversation already. More than once." Probably averaging out to once a week. "I appreciate your concern about my being in a relationship with a man who is Muslim, and I appreciate your concern about my marital status. In fact, I've always appreciated your concern about my marital status. I need you to let go of worrying about it. Everything is fine."

"Who said I was talking about marriage? What's this marital status? I just ask an innocent question about Christmas dinner, and here you are, off talking about marriage. And then you'll blame me for it. This is what always happens. Did I say anything about marriage?"

"You might as well have—"

"Did I say anything about marriage? I did not. I didn't ask you anything. I am merely trying to be civil."

"If Ali's name were John Peterson and he lived up the road from you, you wouldn't be using the word civil," I interrupted. Enough is enough. "The word civil comes in when you feel superior to whomever you're talking about."

"I should hope," my mother said acidly, "that we can all be civil to each other."

"I give up. I give up, Ma. I'm hanging up the phone."

"Don't you hang up like that on me, Sydney Ellen Riley, or I swear—"

I never knew what she swore. I felt like jumping into the harbor and drowning. Or, alternately, pushing her into the harbor and drowning her.

And all this meant was I missed Ali more. I'd come to close to losing him not so very long ago that the tightness I was feeling in my throat was way too familiar, the sense of dread too immediate. He'd been shot once; he could be shot again. Without thinking about what I was doing, I pressed his icon and, of course, got the undercover department's official voicemail. Standard issue. "Please leave a message and it will be delivered to the agent in the field. Thank you."

I didn't realize I was crying until I spoke. "Hi. This message is for Ali Hakim. Ali. It's me. Um, Sydney. I just—I know, I didn't expect you to answer, I don't think you're even hearing this, it's okay, I just miss you so much. I just—" what can anybody say? —I just wish you were here. I love you. Bye."

He was using a different phone, of course. Undercovers don't take anything into the field that can identify them. Someone official would be checking this voicemail, someone who could sort out which messages were truly urgent, like a parent dying, and which could wait, like a lonely girlfriend. He might not even be told I'd been calling, though for sure he'd assume.

I didn't know much about the job. I knew it had something to do with his being fluent in Arabic. I knew it had to do with girls. I knew it was something that would give him nightmares long after it was over. I knew it could end with him getting killed—there's big money in human trafficking, and anywhere there's big money, there's danger. And I knew that at some level I felt some responsibility for what he was doing, because when we first met, Ali was busting people for illicit green-card marriages. I thought that was a perfectly horrible way to spend one's life, and told him so, and it wasn't long before he was asking for a transfer into ICE's Human Trafficking division.

I didn't know he'd do it; it must have been on his mind for a while, because Ali isn't the kind of person to make decisions based on someone else's opinions, even someone he'd unexpectedly fallen in love with. What I did know was I felt morally a lot more comfortable with what he was doing now—and, emotionally, a lot less so. Fraudulent marriages are one thing; people with guns and something to lose are something else altogether.

I thought about calling Karen, his sister, but I was going to have to feel a lot less vulnerable if I did that. Karen and I had a history, and we'd left each other over the summer in an uneasy truce. Besides, what would I say? Has he called you? I wanted her to say yes so I'd know he was okay; I didn't want her to say yes because it would mean she rated above me.

Oh, yes, I can be as childish as the next girl, can't I?

In the meantime, if he didn't come back in time for Christmas, it meant my mother wouldn't have the chance to interrogate him over the opening of presents and the inn's brilliant Christmas dinner, and that was excellent. If he knew I'd invited them, he'd probably have run back to Undercover in no time at all. And I couldn't blame him. My mother was bad enough with me, but we were related; I was stuck with her. For Ali to sit and be polite while she carried on was approaching superhuman.

I sighed. All this was getting me nowhere. Maybe everybody was right; maybe what I needed was a new mystery to solve.

It seemed that P'town was offering me a choice of them.

9

The Lighting of the Pilgrim Monument is a time-honored tradition in town. It's supposed to remind us of Province-town's illustrious history—very few people know, after all, that the Mayflower sailed into Provincetown Harbor, albeit accidentally, after its perilous crossing, or that the Pilgrims first set up shop here, or that the Mayflower Compact was signed here. They all left, Pilgrims and "strangers" alike, and went off to Plymouth once they found there wasn't much drinking water available on a sandbar like the Outer Cape, but even if the history books don't re-member, around here we do.

And not all for good, either.

Guy Husband picked me up right on the dot of four-thirty and there was indeed a parking space at the monument and museum, which saved a cold walk up the hill. We sat in his warm SUV with, for me, a strong sense of déjà vu, waiting for the parking lot to fill in and the festivities to begin. I loved the heated seats. The Little Green Car doesn't have heated seats. "Tell me more about the Mignonette," I urged, none too subtly.

He wasn't going there. "It's your turn," he said. "Tell me about the Mayflower."

I shrugged. Fair is, after all, fair. "Okay. They came here first, is all," I said. "They were way off course, I think they were aiming for Virginia or someplace like that, and this is where they ended up."

"And signed the Mayflower Compact," said Guy.

I nodded. "The precursor to American law," I said. "But things went really bad, really fast. Starting with Dorothy Bradford."

He frowned "There's a pub on Commercial Street called the Governor Bradford," he said.

I nodded. "Named for her husband. First governor of the Commonwealth of Massachusetts," I said.

"What went wrong with her?" he asked.

I relished this story. Talk about a mystery! "So the passage was horrible," I said. "I don't know how you got here from England, but you'd really have to have been driven to do what they did. There were storms. It took sixty-six days. Not enough decent food to eat, everyone sick half the time, worried the next storm would be the last. The ship pitching or rolling or whatever ships do in storms." His department, not mine. "And then they get here finally and anchor in the nice calm harbor, and that's when Dorothy Bradford manages to slip off the deck and drown. She managed to stay on quite nicely throughout all that time at sea, and then slips at anchor?" I sketched quotation marks around the word slips.

"What do you think happened to her? Did she kill herself?"

"Pfft. Why wait? Why not do it at sea? The Cape couldn't have looked that dismal," I said. "It was all forested then, not like it is now. There were huge trees, but over time settlers took them all down for building and for ships' masts and to send back to England to the corporations that financed their trips." I was getting off-topic, but I imagined it sometimes, the Cape green and filled with growth, lush and filled with secret glens and hollows.

Guy brought me back to the conversation. "So Dorothy Bradford—"

"What do you think?" I asked rhetorically. "I think she was murdered."

He thought about it for a moment. "The governor?"

I shrugged. "He remarried," I said.

"Not sure that's an indictment."

Maybe. "Anyway," I went on, "no one was behaving particularly well. Oh, yeah, they wrote the Compact, bully for them, but they also were at the cutting edge of white people coming and, quote-unquote, *discovering* a whole place that—

surprise, surprise—already had a perfectly good civilization and way of life going."

"The native Americans," said Guy, nodding.

"The Wampanoag," I said.

"It couldn't have been too bad," he said, "if they didn't stay."

My eyes widened. "Couldn't have been too bad?" I repeated. "Okay, you go up into the museum there, and you'll see a charming little diorama about these people. And you'll see that winter was drawing in and they didn't have enough to eat—they'd already consumed everything from the trip, I don't know what they expected to find here, but what they found was a Cape Cod winter. But—guess what! A bunch of the men were off on a little trip looking for fresh water, and surprise, surprise, they came upon a whole bunch of corn, neatly stacked and stored. Hallelujah! They found the corn! God was truly looking out for them!"

Guy said, mildly, "I take it this corn belonged to the—what did you say the tribe's name was?"

"Wampanoag," I said. "I don't know about you, but where I come from, what they did is called stealing. That was for the tribe's winter, not for the Europeans. And now in this country we tell our kids this lovely fable about everyone having a sumptuous meal together and getting along."

There were people streaming by us to go up to the celebration. "I'll get off my soapbox now," I said. "Come on, let's go light this monument."

He was looking at me oddly, but I didn't have time to figure out what his expression meant. We went through the museum itself—we'd be back later for the cider and the music and to warm up—and out back to stand and look up at the monument. It's modeled after a church tower in Italy that has no connection whatsoever with Provincetown, but oh well.

I kept bumping into people I knew—Vernon Porter, dressed to the nines as his alter-ego Lady Di, and Will from Days Propane, and Julie Knapp from Twisted Pizza. Mirela was there, and Thea with her new girlfriend Claudia, and John Silva. Mike from the inn looked like he was going to perish from the cold, which seems odd when you think that his hobby is fishing, and he's out in all sorts of weather; even Glenn, talking with the town manager and a couple of the Cape political luminaries who had come to make speeches. I hoped they weren't discussing commercial real estate prices.

Mirela was onto Guy in a heartbeat. I'd slipped my arm through his—it was cold, and it seemed the thing to do, no meaning in the gesture—but she took one look at it and linked her arm though his on the other side. I don't know if she was defending Ali *in absentium*, expressing interest in Guy, or possibly both. "This is the first time you have come to the Lighting," she informed him, looking up through silky lashes. Oh, *really*, Mirela. She's one of the few people in town whose sexual preference is ambiguous— most of us are pretty clear one way or another— and while I've known her to have dalliances with women, her go-to preference is men, though she doesn't generally do it as blatantly as this.

He was smiling at her. "It's a beautiful ceremony," he said.

I gaped at him. "I just told you how terrible it is—"

Mirela frowned at me. "You are here, are you not, sunshine? It cannot be too bad."

"That's not—"

"Bulgaria," Guy pronounced. "You're from Bulgaria."

She smiled. "How did you identify my accent so quickly? Or did Sydney tell you?"

"Of course not," I said, and at the same time he smoothly disengaged himself from me and held out his hand for Mirela to shake. "Guy Husband," he said.

Her eyes widened. "No," I put in, "he's not kidding. It really is his name."

She shook his hand. "My name is Mirela," she said, a little breathlessly. Breathlessly? Eww.

"Oh, for heaven's sake," I said. It felt like time had accelerated suddenly, like the lights were all moving just a little too quickly around me, people's conversations speeded up, colors a little too bright and piercing. "I'm going to see if I can find someone sensible to talk to. You two are on your own."

What I couldn't figure out was why I was feeling this sudden stab of jealousy at how Mirela had stepped in so easily, disengaged Guy from me, and claimed him for herself. I was with Ali, wasn't I? I didn't even *know* Guy Husband, did I? It shouldn't matter to me what he got up to with Mirela, or anyone else for that matter.

Besides, he was that kind of perfect-handsome that's usually gay. Besides, I had other things on my mind. Besides, there was Ali.

Speeches were made, the monument's strings of lights were duly lit after an enthusiastic countdown, and everybody converged on the museum building itself, which had the advantage of heat; the wind had picked up—it's always windy on the Cape, but this was ridiculous—and it was a relief to get inside.

I had grabbed a cup of hot cider and was standing with my hands wrapped around it for warmth when the crowd more or less shoved me up against one of the big glass cases lining the walls, this one with artifacts from Provincetown Arctic explorer Donald MacMillan. A hand shot out to help me steady the hot liquid. "There! You don't want to burn yourself."

"Thanks," I said and looked for my benefactor. It was Craig Carlson, one of the assistant harbormasters, his long hair pulled back into a ponytail, wearing a down-filled vest and sensible boots and looking uncomfortably warm in the overheated room. Roger is in charge of the harbormaster's office, but there are several others who work with him year-round, with another three added in the summertime. "Hey, Craig."

"Enjoying the Lighting?" he asked politely. He had sensibly opted only for a cookie.

"I'm enjoying it more now that I'm inside," I said. I looked at him with some speculation. Might as well use my time wisely. "So you know about the thing they found from the Bessie G?" I asked. I wasn't giving anything away; James hadn't asked for discretion, and besides, Craig was one of the assistant harbormasters, and if anyone knew anything, it would be him.

He looked a little startled. "I didn't know it was public knowledge," he said.

I shrugged. "Only as public as me, I guess," I said. "James showed me the photos he took of the board."

Craig looked around. "Helen Correia's here somewhere," he said, lowering his voice. "Maybe we shouldn't talk about it."

"Why, shouldn't she know?" I paused. "Who's Helen Correia?" She wasn't Tony's wife; Tony's wife's name was Sarah, and she had disappeared with the Bessie G.

"Shh," he said, and half-turned from the door. I of course immediately tried to check out who'd just come in, but the room was just too jammed for that, with even more people unbelievably still pouring in, looking for warmth. I turned back to Craig and said, as softly as I could, "Who's Helen Correia?"

"Tony's sister," he said. "She was over at the office yesterday. It shook her up a lot, seein' that photo."

"I should think so." I was still scanning faces over his shoulder; it didn't matter, I didn't know who I was looking for. "What does she think happened?"

He shrugged, took a bite out of his cookie, chewed it pensively. "I think she thought Sarah did it, took the girls and cleared out," he said.

I was startled. "Why?"

"No reason. I mean, no reason she'd have for thinkin' that. But you have to think *something*, don't you? There has to be an explanation. Things don't just disappear. So she thought maybe Sarah was seein' somebody, and they killed Tony together and took off together."

"Someone with a gun," I said.

Craig nodded. "But no one really shared that theory," he said. "No evidence for it. Wasn't nobody in town, that's for sure, couldn't keep a secret like that, right? Sooner or later, you have an affair in this town, everybody an' their brother knows about it. And Sarah never spent time up-Cape, not enough to be seein' anybody, anyway. Oh, you know, she went up to Hyannis for shopping sometimes, up to Trader Joe's or Home Depot or K-Mart or something, just like everybody else, but she usually had the girls with her, and that was all. No, no one thinks there was anybody else. Her and Tony, they were good together. Helen was just looking for reasons."

"Why, didn't she like Sarah?"

"She didn't like not knowing who killed her brother, more like," Craig said. "Who would?"

I sighed and scanned the room again. "So what does she think, now the boat's been found?"

"The boat hasn't been found," he reminded me. "Just part of the stern."

"What, and you think the rest of it's somewhere else?" I demanded. "I don't know much about boats, but I don't expect they go far without the stern." Which was, I thought hopefully, the back of the boat, something one couldn't do without. I really did need to learn more about boats.

"It could be anywhere," Craig said soberly. "Them storms, they bring stuff up from all over the place. You can't tell where something is just from where that shit washes up. Part of it, sure, but it's more complicated than that."

I frowned. Hadn't John said the opposite, the other night at my apartment? "I thought that if you knew the general location of a wreck, and something came up on a certain beach, that would help pinpoint it," I said. "Or at least confirm it."

"Who told you that?" He shook his head, not waiting for an answer. "Too many variables. Wind, tide, lots going on there."

I caught a glimpse of Guy through the crowd and waved. He nodded and said something to someone beside him. "Now there's the man to be," said Craig, following my eyes.

"What does that mean?" The cider was finally cool enough to sip.

"He's got everything, and he gets to go after pirate treasure on top of it all," said Craig. "Come on, Sydney! Every little boy wants to grow up to be a pirate! And goin' after pirate treasure, that has to be the next-best thing." He nodded over my shoulder. "Looks like I get to do the next-best thing to that, meet the man himself."

Guy was indeed making his way over to us, and Mirela was still with him. I didn't have time to deconstruct Craig's sarcasm. "Well, you were right, it was a splendid sight, seeing the Lighting," Guy said to me, then put out his hand to Craig. "Hello, there. Guy Husband," he said.

Craig had finished his cookie, but he still made a point of brushing off the crumbs from his down vest before taking Guy's hand. What was that about? "Craig Carlson," he said.

Guy nodded. "I believe I saw you in the harbormaster's office recently," he said, and drew Mirela closer into the conversation. "You know each other?" He was getting used to being in a small town.

"Sure," said Craig easily. "Hey, Mirela."

"Did you enjoy the Lighting?" Mirela asked him, her expression showing nothing but polite interest. I felt we were in the middle of a Renaissance dance. Step forward, step back. Turn to your right.

My turn to join in. I said to Guy, "Craig and I were just talking about how exciting your work must be." Sydney Riley, specialist in small-talk, inane chatter while you wait.

"Well, there are a lot of months of rather uninteresting research," Guy said, self-deprecating. "Sometimes years, actually. But we're hoping for a good result here."

"Craig was telling me there's no more news about that fishing boat," I went on, undeterred by what had sounded like finality in his voice. I might not know much about boats, but I know you can't fish without putting bait in the water.

Even if you don't know exactly what it is you're fishing for.

Guy's attention went from zero to a hundred in three seconds flat. "Yes, indeed, the harbormaster was telling me about that," he said. "What a terrible accident."

"Which harbormaster?" asked Craig, a little truculence seeping into his voice. "I'm harbormaster, too." Oh, great, just when there's a chance of getting some real information, we're off to a pissing contest.

"Of course you are," said Guy smoothly, glossing over his misstep. "I was speaking to

Roger; I don't believe I met you there. No offence intended whatever." He paused, delicately. "Tell me, has there been any more news of the fishing boat? What is the name—the Bessie? Do they think it might be salvageable?"

"The Bessie G," I said.

"It's more salvage you're looking for?" asked Craig. He definitely didn't like Guy. "I'd've thought you'd have your hands full with your pirate ship out there."

"Anything we can do to help," said Guy smoothly. "As it happens, one of my salvage vessels is quite close by, just in Boston at the moment. I can have it here in hours, if that could be helpful in any way."

Boston? If John had only called Guy recently—and hadn't he been in Scotland?—how did he have a salvage ship in Boston already? Even I knew those things don't turn on a dime.

Craig was still being aggressive. "And what kind of salvage exactly you think you're getting from a fishing boat?"

Guy opened his mouth to respond, and Mirela made some sort of small gesture, a movement really, but her intent was telegraphed loud and clear: *be careful.*

Craig was starting to look murderous, and Guy more and more baffled. I was feeling a little baffled myself, but what this Lighting didn't need was an all-out scuffle. I put a hand on Guy's arm. "You have to remember," I said. "Around here, something that recent? A wreck like that, it's a grave. People in this room loved people on that boat."

"Of course," said Guy. "Of course. And if called upon to help… well, we would only treat it with the utmost respect. Absolutely. But it might be helpful to have—what is the word you use? Closure?"

"We'll take care of our own closure," said Craig. It came out as a growl. "Don't need nobody from outside to do it for us."

"Of course," Guy said again. "I wouldn't presume—"

"Then don't."

I exchanged a look with Mirela. *How about them Red Sox?* Mirela said, brightly, "We are going back to your inn, Sydney, for a drink. Will you come with us? Craig as well?"

Craig brushed himself off again, the gesture totally unnecessary and clearly symbolic "Not me," he said. "Got an early start in the morning. Family's coming here for Thanksgiving, Brenda'll kill me if I don't get the turkey in the oven in time."

"I'm sure we'll see each other again," Guy said to him. "It was a pleasure meeting you. Have a happy holiday."

We watched him shoulder his way toward the door away from us. "Well," Mirela said once he was out of earshot, "perhaps he is not feeling the Thanksgiving spirit. That is a pity."

"You're from Bulgaria," I said to her. "Exactly what Thanksgiving spirit are you talking about?"

She looked hurt. "I love Thanksgiving," she said. And it's true: Mirela has embraced everything American with open arms. You should see what she does for the Fourth of July. "I know that you do not, sunshine, but perhaps you can *not* think about the history, and think about the gratitude instead?"

"Mirela—" Guy said, but I headed him off. "You don't have to be polite," I said, glaring at Mirela. "This is a conversation we have every year. We're never going to resolve it."

"You do not celebrate the holiday?" he asked, arching an eyebrow.

I shook my head. "I told you before," I said. I was feeling cross and still unsettled. About learning that Guy had a research vessel already in the area. About the way Guy and Mirela were clinging to each other. Not sure why any of it was bothering me so much. "I don't celebrate genocides."

Mirela rolled her eyes. "So nice. You are nothing but fun tonight, sunshine," she observed, then touched Guy's arm and spoke directly to him. "We should leave, it is so stuffy in here."

Why don't we go someplace that's quieter? Talk about a pick-up line.

Guy turned to me. "Are you ready? If you don't wish to come to the inn, then I'm happy to drop you off." He said to Mirela, "Sydney and I came up the hill together."

"It's fine," I snapped. Mirela was right about one thing: it was indeed getting stuffy, too many people in their winter gear in just a few rooms. Big rooms, but still. The music was starting to get louder and that was only making things worse. "I'll walk. I could use the air."

Guy looked concerned. "Are you sure? Because—"

I flapped a hand at him, suddenly exhausted. "It's fine," I said again. "It's downhill from here." Literally, in fact.

Mirela let go of Guy long enough to hug me. "I will call you," she promised.

I relented. "Happy Thanksgiving, Mirela." I disengaged from her hug and offered my hand to Guy. "Happy Thanksgiving," I said. "Welcome to America."

But I wondered, even as I slipped through the crowd and buttoned up my coat, exactly what Guy was here for.

10

Of course I'd forgotten I was going to go to Thea and Claudia's house after the Lighting. To enjoy a very good wine. One of these days I'll get an app on my phone that keeps me from forgetting things.

Or maybe I'd just get a new brain. The one I had felt a little tired.

I called Thea on Thanksgiving morning and left an apologetic voicemail message. They'd probably already gone wherever they were going for the holiday. I had the Little Green Car back, but there was nowhere I really wanted to go.

The Race Point Inn does Thanksgiving well—we have guests who reserve their places at the tables year after year after year—in a classic but elegant way. Adrienne the diva chef doesn't lower herself to turkey and stuffing; that's left to the sous-chef du jour—Adrienne goes through sous-chefs like I go through chocolate—and she instead creates side-dishes so amazing that Food and Wine magazine once did a special on them alone. I'm always invited, of course, and I've gone occasionally, especially when there's an event attached to it; we once had a double wedding along with the Thanksgiving feast. Barry loved, loved, *loved* Thanksgiving.

This Thanksgiving, though, with the future of the inn up in the air and my missing Ali and my unsettled feelings about everything else going on, I just didn't want to be there. An early-morning call from Mirela had confirmed that she and Guy would both be spending the day at the inn, as they had the previous night, and that was something else I didn't want to think about.

I ended up spending the day in my pajamas, curled up in bed with Ibsen purring madly at my side, drinking cup after cup of hot cocoa until I felt quite sick, and re-reading my way solidly through two books from Tana French's detective series. Maybe I was looking for inspiration.

As though there were something here to detect that I was missing. Had Glenn made up his mind? Was Ali ever coming back? Who shot Tony Correia? Had Guy Husband really found a missing pirate ship? What was his research ship doing in Boston Harbor? Was the Bessie G somewhere out there?

I finally gave it up, took a long hot shower, cooked an omelet and ate half of it, and went to bed for good. Another Thanksgiving bites the dust.

A Fatal Folly

The Saturday after Thanksgiving is the second in the series of iconic Provincetown events leading up to our beloved Holly Folly: the lighting of the lobster pot tree.

It's not really a tree, of course. It's actually over a hundred lobster traps—or "pots," as they're known—stacked over two stories high and decorated with garlands, bright red bows, and thousands of lights. The pots are real ones, on loan for the season by local fishermen. There's a crane that comes and puts the last pot on the top. While not as popular as the Lighting of the monument, it still draws a lot of people, and we all cheer and sing and it's generally pretty festive.

I wasn't about to let my bad mood get in the way of enjoying it.

The "tree" in in the center of Lopes Square, right where MacMillan Pier ends; in the summertime the square is filled with tourists coming in off the ferries or heading out for a boat ride; most of the storefronts lining it are hot-dog, ice-cream, and fried-clam takeaway joints, closed now. In the center are a few well-tended trees, benches, rubbish and recycling bins, and a large anchor of dubious provenance. That's where the lobster-pot tree goes.

I got to the square in plenty of time to chat; it's another social occasion, and for once there wasn't too much of a wind to make you wish you lived anywhere but on a tiny spit of land in the Atlantic Ocean. I was well-insulated against the cold. It felt good to get out of the apartment; I'd been cooped up with my own thoughts for too long.

Thea grabbed me right away. "Sydney! We missed you the other night!"

"I know," I said. "I'm so sorry, sweetie. I just completely spaced it." Well, there was forgetting… and then there was being too busy trying to puzzle out problems that weren't really mine to begin with. Two days spent indoors reading hadn't brought illumination to any of the questions bothering me; Tana French's detectives had penetrating thoughts and asked penetrating questions, and I was just running around doing my best imitation of a goldfish. I was ready to call detecting quits.

"You missed some nice wine," she said. "It's fine; don't look like that! It really was fine. Our neighbors came back with us, and everybody ended up staying up way too late. We played Scrabble."

"I'm glad," I said. I really was; I can be sarcastic, I know, but I'm not actually usually rude. I felt bad that they were probably watching the door for half that Scrabble game. "I do feel bad."

Her eyes were sparkling wickedly. "I have something that can help," she said. "Here," and she slipped a nip bottle into my hand—cinnamon-spiked whisky. I took a swallow and could feel it warming me all the way down, shooting into my stomach and my chest and my limbs. I grinned.

She giggled, happy as a child. "We brought a whole bunch of them," she said mischievously. "Better than hot cider."

Everyone else was drinking hot chocolate, served in Styrofoam cups; and they'd already started singing the Christmas carols. You could see people's breath in the frigid air. I gave it my all, banishing thoughts of Glenn and Barry, of my mother, of ships and shipwrecks. God rest ye merry, gentlemen, indeed. Thea passed me another bottle and I took another nip. Definitely feeling in the spirit now.

And then across the square, the lights dancing in the air between us, I caught sight of Mirela and Guy. He had his arm around her shoulder and she was laughing, and all at once the singing receded, the warmth of the alcohol and Thea's arm linked through mine receded, the bright lights and the Currier-and-Ives feeling receded and it was suddenly too much for me, the absence beside me, the emptiness I kept pushing to the back of my mind. I could almost feel Ali's arm around me, could hear him whispering something funny and sardonic into my ear, could remember last year's lobster tree lightning when we'd gone back to my apartment and put up my very small Christmas tree—yes, Ma, Ali does celebrate certain aspects of Christmas—and I'd drunk a very lovely Chianti that Glenn had given me (Ali's observant enough to neither drink nor smoke), and we'd stayed in bed the whole next day.

I didn't know where he was. I didn't know what he was doing. It might have been innocuous, a business deal he had to pretend to go through with, container ships he had to watch. Middle Eastern potentates negotiating for modern-day harems in business suits and boardrooms. Or maybe not. Maybe undercover work included getting involved with a woman.

Maybe it involved getting shot.

It was all just too much. I pulled my arm away, squeezed Thea's elbow, and made my way out of the crowd. To my enormous disgust, I was in full-fledged crying mode. I meant to go down the pier and look at the fleet tied up there—some of the boats are always lighted, and there are piercingly strong lights on the pier itself, it really can be an Instagram-worthy sight—but there were people blocking the way and so instead I stumbled into the big municipal parking lot, now only about a quarter full.

Once I'd started in that direction, I kept on, threading through the cars and out into the empty stretch farther back, cursing myself for not having tissues in my pocket (who the hell carries tissues in her pocket, anyway?). At the end of the parking lot is a walkway that fronts the water, with a couple of benches; it's pretty in summer and a favorite dog-walking path. My plan by then was to sit down, finish my second nip (which probably had a great deal to do with the tears), and get a hold of myself.

Instead, I tripped—quite literally—over a corpse.

***

There are a lot of things that normal people would say if they found themselves on a frozen path next to a frozen body. I can imagine some of them. I didn't say any of those things. What I said was, "I don't *believe* this!"

Seriously. I'm absolutely sorry for the fellow and everything, but this was carrying the *Murder, She Wrote* analogy just a little too far. My life was complicated and getting more complicated by the minute, and damn it, Scott Coffey was right. If there was a body anywhere in Provincetown, I was going to be the one to find it.

Then, of course, I came to my senses. A dead guy. Well, a body, anyway. Maybe I should actually do something about it, instead of sitting here thinking finding him was all about me.

I finally struggled to a sitting position so I could see if he was in fact dead—if this were an overdose or he'd passed out drunk, then I needed to move quickly to get help—and immediately pain shot up from my ankle. Frosting on the cake.

There might not have been any cake to be frosted, but there was certainly frost on *him*: regardless of how this man had died, it had clearly already happened., and some time ago. I know because I grabbed his arm when I got off-balance from the ankle, and it was stiff as a board.

Stiff as a board off the Bessie G. Under the sodium vapor light above us, and once I could focus, I managed to make out who it was. I knew him. His name was Pete Teller, he was another wintertime assistant harbormaster, and you couldn't tell me this was all unrelated.

It was going to be a very long night.

11

I'm not even going to pretend to be sur-prised," Julie Agassi was saying. She's the chief of detectives in Provincetown, and a friend. And we'd done this dance together be-fore.

"It really *was* an accident," I said. "I mean, not him being dead, I don't know if that's an accident or not, but me finding him? That really was an accident. Totally."

My teeth were chattering and I'd have given anything for another of Thea's nips, though the two I'd had were turning sour on me. I really hoped I wasn't going to throw up.

We were sitting on one of the benches along the pathway, inside the police tape that had gone up quickly, unobtrusively. There was a crowd of people on the other side of it, craning their necks to get a better view; they were get-ting a lot more than their money's worth at this year's lobster pot tree lighting.

Julie sighed. "So, okay, let's do this again," she said. "You left Lopes Square—why?"

Why? Because I was lonely and feeling sorry for myself. Because my mother was coming for Christmas, my boyfriend was gone, my job was in jeopardy. No wonder I was fixating on shipwrecks. "I was crying," I said to Julie. "I didn't want people to see me crying."

She frowned, her pen poised over her pad of paper. Julie had the investigation only until the state police arrived from their headquarters in South Yarmouth: in Massachusetts, they're the investigative arm of the district attorney, and they're the ones in charge of all homicides. The fact that I actually *know* this bit of arcane information says everything about how ridiculous my life was feeling right at that moment.

"Why did you come here? I mean, here, specifically?"

I sighed. "I was going to go down the pier," I said, using the local expression. "I was going to look at the boats—you know, something that wasn't all happy and Christmas-y. I didn't want to run into anyone I knew." Nice job doing that, Riley. Your choice of words is inspired. I took a deep breath. "But I kind of went off in a tangent into the parking lot."

"Why?"

"I don't know!" Exasperation made my voice sharp. "Honestly, Julie, I don't know. There were some people standing between me and the pier, they were singing, and I just *did.*"

The path connected to the pier; I might have had some idea about wandering that way. I was telling the truth: I really didn't know. And then I thought since that's where I was, anyway, I'd just sit come over and here."

"In the cold." It wasn't a question.

"Not for long," I said. "I didn't bring a *picnic* or anything."

Her expression was not one of amusement. I can't help it; fear brings out the sarcasm. She cleared her throat. "And you tripped over something."

I nodded. "Literally," I said miserably. "Do you know how long he'd been there?" I was starting to feel bad about that. We'd all been a few hundred feet away, laughing and singing and doing all the joyous things one does for a holiday Pete Teller wasn't going to celebrate ever again.

"Okay," she said, bundling her notebook back into her uniform jacket and ignoring my question. "They'll probably want to talk to you at some point, but you don't have to stay here now, they know where you live." That's reassuring: the state police know where I live. Julie paused. "Is Ali in town?"

I shook my head. "He's in California."

"Okay," she said again, her voice brisk. "We'll find Mirela. Go home, get warm." She was gesturing to one of the other cops standing at the perimeter; they'd called everybody in. "Celia, can you see that Sydney gets home?"

"No, I'm fine," I said. What I didn't want was to have to talk to anybody, much less arrive at my home in a police cruiser. The club downstairs would be open by now, and I didn't need to be the object of speculation. "Really, Julie. I'd rather be alone."

"She can drop you at the corner," Julie said, accurately diagnosing the problem but not giving in. "Come on," urged Celia, and I got up reluctantly. "Do you know what happened to him?" I asked Julie.

"No," she said. "And I wouldn't tell you if I did."

Celia was as good as Julie's word; she didn't pull right up to my house, but stopped the cruiser on Bradford Street, put on the blue lights. Okay, maybe discretion wasn't their key skill. "Thanks," I said.

"Get warm," she said, and then added, quickly, "Sydney, listen to me a moment. You're going want to go in and drink alcohol; don't do it. It's a natural reaction, but it's only going to make things worse. Take a hot shower, drink some tea, try to relax."

I resisted a ridiculous impulse to apologize. "Goodnight," I said instead. I could feel her watching me as I walked down the hill to my house. There was a strong bass-beat coming from the club and the stairs had never felt so steep, so numerous.

The light was on, the heat was on, and John was sitting on the sofa, rubbing a delighted

Ibsen. I sighed, shut the door, and leaned against it. "I'm going to have to seriously start locking my door," I said.

"Why?" he asked. "You don't have anything to steal. You don't even have much of anything to *eat*. When's the last time you went to the Stop & Shop?"

I pushed myself off the door and made it as far as the one armchair that doesn't look like it came from the thrift store. "I'm so sorry," I said as sarcastically as I could manage. "Am I forgetting something? Did I invite you for dinner?"

"Nope. But I got hungry, waiting."

"Ah," I said, nodding wisely. "And now we're going to come to the evening's featured presentation, the reason you're here. And it had better be entertaining, 'cause I've just had one hell of a night."

"I saw that," John said. "You were the one found Pete Teller."

"I am, strangely enough, already aware of that fact," I said. "John. Come to the point."

"You don't want to drink alcohol," he said.

"Oh, for heaven's sake!" I was cold and tired and not in the mood. "I wish people would stop telling me that. What am I, the town lush?" If I were trying for the title, I'd have some stiff competition. Provincetown is as far east as you can get—the next stop is Portugal, three thousand miles away. What that means is no one gets here by accident. We're not on the way anywhere else; no one stopped here along the way.

The kind of people attracted to Land's End are crazy, creative, and occasionally very damaged. Most of the town's retail establishments shut down in the off-season; we have three liquor stores that stay open and thriving all year round. You do the math.

"I'm just looking out for you," John said, looking hurt.

"Good. If that's what you came to say, you've said it. Thanks for the visit, thanks for the concern, and now you're on your way."

"Mirela called me," he said. "She said you shouldn't be alone."

Oh, my God. Was there anyone in Provincetown that Mirela wasn't asking to keep an eye on me these days? "And she's too busy with the new boyfriend to keep me company, I suppose." The words were out before I could even formulate them in my head. I think we both looked a little shocked. "I didn't mean it like that," I said.

"I know," said John. "She's worried about you, is all."

"Well, I'm okay," I said. "You can tell her that. I'm cold and shaken and I just need to warm up."

John showed no signs of leaving. "So, Pete Teller," he said. "Can't say I'm completely surprised."

"You're not? I'm surprised as hell," I said. For a place that usually counts three bicycle thefts as a crime wave, this is a little excessive.

"Not him getting killed," agreed John. "Just him getting killed, if you know what I mean."

I blinked. "No," I said. "I have absolutely no idea what you mean."

"You ever see his house?"

"No. We're not—we weren't—besties, or anything like that." I decided that following the conversation might be the best way to get him out of my apartment as expediently as possible. "Why?"

"I looked it up on Zillow," said John. "He got it for a million point two."

"Okay," I said cautiously. "So he's got a nice house." It probably wasn't going to console his widow any. If he was married. I knew nothing about him other than he worked at the harbormaster's office. Once when Thea and I had rented a boat from Flyer's he'd come round on one of the harbormaster's boats, blue lights flashing, to tell us to get the hell out of the shipping lane. We told him we would if we knew how—we were totally becalmed—and he threw us a rope and towed us out.

"So what he's got is a house he couldn't afford on what he takes home from the town," said John. "His salary's public record."

"Again," I said, "maybe you can make a point here?"

He sighed. "All I'm saying is, I'm thinking he might have been involved in stuff he shouldn't. Stuff that gets you killed."

I was finally following along. And I remembered a Portuguese Festival not so long ago when I'd realized that gunrunning wasn't only a thing, it was a thing that happened here. "So this is a border patrol issue?"

"Not guns," said John. "Drugs."

I laughed; I actually laughed. I must have been more tired, or closer to hysteria, than I'd realized. "They don't bring in drugs here," I said.

He looked at me. "You're not serious," he said.

I gestured halfheartedly. "Oh, come on, this is Provincetown," I said. He just kept looking at me. I tried again. "All I've heard about in the news lately are stories about fentanyl," I said. "And I'm pretty sure that's coming from China. Cape Cod is a kind of roundabout way to get something here from China." I got up, finally, and went to the stove. "I'm putting on the kettle for tea," I said. "Are you staying?"

He made a face. "I hate tea," he said. "Don't you have nothing stronger?"

"I thought I wasn't supposed to drink," I said.

"Don't mean I can't," he replied.

"Aren't you going to meetings? Last time you were here, you said you were. I thought you weren't drinking anymore."

"Not drinking *beer*," he said.

I shrugged and got the bottle of Jamieson's from the cupboard. I wasn't the abstinence police. "Don't think the irony of discussing one illegal drug while partaking of a legal one has escaped me," I said.

He ignored me, came over, located a glass, rinsed it, and put a half-inch of whiskey in it before going back to the sofa. "Anyway," he said, "That's not the point. Fentanyl ain't what people go out and buy. Not around here, anyway."

All I seemed to have were herbal teas. I was so not in the mood for herbal tea. "Then what?"

"Heroin." He wasn't drinking, just holding the glass. "And it don't come from China."

I finally found the good tea, hiding behind the bags of Sleepytime. "From where, then?"

"Mexico." He set the whiskey, untouched, onto the coffee table. "Used to come up from the south, over the land border. Not anymore. Now most of the heroin in the country's coming through New England." He caught my glance. "What? I'm not supposed to know shit? Look it up if you don't believe me. Ask your friends at the police station. Why'd you think there's so much heroin use in the mill towns? It comes in here. Here, an' New Bedford, an' Gloucester."

"By boat?"

He peered at me. "And they actually gave you a college degree and everything?"

"It could have been airplanes," I said defensively. "Sue me; I'm not at my best tonight."

I didn't ask him how he knew so much about it; like I said, we have a lot of people in town who are pretty clear about where their next meal is coming from, and it isn't the Stop & Shop. My mother talks a lot about how many overdoses there are in New Hampshire, even in the rarefied air of her particular community, where genteel residents start with prescribed Percocet and move on from there. Clusters of use—and subsequent overdoses—are all over New England.

But *P'town?*

John was watching me. "Just because you don't see it, don't mean it's not here," he said. "You see what you let yourself see, Sydney."

The teakettle whistled and I took it off the gas and poured hot water into the teapot. The warm smoky odor of Lapsang Souchong filled the air. I've been accused of being oblivious before. It might even be true. I knew that three people can walk down Commercial Street and "see" three different layers of existence: different people, different venues, different small signs and gestures that only they can read. It doesn't just happen here; it happens everywhere. Just ask any two people who grew up in the same family—they didn't grow up in the same family.

All I knew was I was exhausted, and for once I wanted to be anywhere but where I was. Generally I'm pretty happy being in Provincetown: it's like living inside a postcard. Right now I'd like to be miles away. Tahiti, maybe. Being served blue drinks with fruit and little umbrellas in them. "So Pete could have been an over-dose," I said, carrying the teapot and a cup over to the armchair.

"Coulda," acknowledged John. He still hadn't drunk any of the Jamieson's. "Don't know. Didn't *think* he was using, but you never know."

I dragged my attention back. I'd been forgetting the import business and Pete's million-dollar home. "Or it could have been financial," I said. "He could have gotten in trouble with someone if he was really bringing heroin in." It was a great cover, actually, working for the harbormaster. You were allowed to go anywhere at any time, and the Coast Guard would probably pretty much leave you alone unless they had a very good reason not to.

"Coulda," said John again. "Point it, it could be anything, but my money's on something he shouldn't of been doing. Your heat doing okay now?"

"What?" I looked up, startled, from pouring my tea. "The heat's fine," I said.

"Good." He stood up. "Should get going."

He hadn't told me why he'd been there in the first place. He hadn't said why he wanted a glass of whiskey he wasn't going to drink. I was too tired to ask him any questions. I flapped a hand in his direction. "Okay."

Please God, don't let anything else happen tonight.

Nothing did.

A week and a half passed with no news on any front. The investigator from the state police, someone new named McCall (and why I should even know the previous one was the biggest mystery of all), confirmed my story about literally tripping over the body. He clearly thought I was holding something back and I suggested he have a conversation with Julie, or his predecessor, or both, if he wanted to establish my bona fides. He was unamused.

Nothing new there. I haven't yet met anyone who works for the state police who has a sense of humor.

Mirela resurfaced in her studio, working madly toward her Holly Folly deadline. Guy Husband was spending a lot of time in the inn's dining-room, drinking pots of English tea and huddled on the telephone, looking at maps and printouts spread around him on the table; or so Mike reported.

Glenn didn't make any decisions.

Ali remained silent and out of reach. I was starting to be convinced something had happened to him. I'd taken to pulling out his clothing from the drawer it inhabited in my dressed and smelling it, hoping to catch his cologne, his scent. *Pathetic, Riley.*

My mother called no less than four times, with increasing levels of hysteria. She clearly didn't believe that I wasn't in touch with Ali. "You may as well tell me the truth, Sydney, you know I always find out. He's staying away because of me, isn't he? The moment you invited your father and I—"

"Ma, it's not about you. He's working. On the west coast. In California. On something important." Or so I had to continue believing. Ali does actually save lives, beside which the wedding business seems small potatoes indeed. I tried again. "It has nothing to do with you." That was patently ridiculous: my mother believes that everything inside the parameters of the Milky Way relates to her in one way or another.

"But he'll come home for the holidays, won't he? Those people must celebrate *something* in December. Everyone does."

Actually, the only Islamic holiday remotely corresponding to winter is the Prophet's birthday—but that's a moveable feast and can occur anywhere from October to December, depending on the year. I wasn't about to try and explain that to my mother. Nor did I have the energy to address her racism; that would be a conversation without end and one that would make me wish she'd move to Alaska. Except that they still have phones in Alaska. And Inuit. She'd probably be as racist about the Inuit as she was about Muslims. I was going to suddenly change her mind? "I don't know when he's coming back, Ma."

"But he'll surely want to come back for Christmas—for the holidays!" That's Ma being politically correct, changing "Christmas" to "holidays." "And when he does, you'll want him to be with us, won't you? We'll have to let the inn know. We're having Christmas dinner at the inn, aren't we? I can't see you cooking in that place of yours. So we need to know if he'll be there."

We were having an argument about a non-event that was rapidly assuming mythical proportions, both in importance and in the probability that it would never happen. "Can we just wait and see? Please?"

She sniffed. My mother hasn't waited to see about anything, ever. "You're starting to take an attitude with me, Sydney," she said, a note of menace dropping into her voice. "I'm just trying to make things as smooth and pleasant as possible. I don't understand why you feel a need to take an attitude."

Breathe, Riley. "Ma," I said, as calmly as I could manage, "taking an attitude is the least I can do, with everything happening in my life right now. Please hear me. I'm looking forward to you and Dad coming down. If by some miracle Ali is free by then, he'll join us. You'll stay at the inn and he'll stay at my place. Whatever happens, will happen. It'll all work out."

There was a moment of silence while she considered her next angle of attack. I have it on good authority that my mother is a reincarnation of one of Napoleon's generals. "John Curtis came here for Thanksgiving," she said.

Wait, what? Why was she talking about *Thanksgiving?* "Okay," I said helplessly.

"You know exactly who I'm talking about. He was engaged to Marti Sullivan's daughter," my mother went on. "But they broke it off."

Now I saw where this was going. "I'm not interested in John Curtis," I said. I still had absolutely no idea who he was. I had no idea who Marti Sullivan, or her daughter, were. I cared even less. "I have a boyfriend." Even if "boyfriend" sounds a little *jejune* for someone in her mid-thirties. "I know you'll find this hard to believe, but I'm happy." Well, okay, that wasn't quite accurate in the particulars, but it held up for my life in general.

"If things were going so well, he wouldn't have left you alone to go out to California," my mother said.

Oh, God. I really was going to have to kill her.

12

December arrived, and with it the much-anticipated start of Holly Folly: Souper Saturday.

It's a benefit for Provincetown's venerable soup kitchen, which feeds hundreds of people over the winter, so the "good cause" box can be ticked off. But it's also great fun. Fifteen or twenty local restaurants—many of which have already closed for the season—show up with soups to sample: clam chowder from the Canteen, fennel bisque from Ross' Grill, chicken soup with Thai and Mexican peppers from the Mews, squid stew from the Lobster Pot… every year there's something different and amazing. I never miss a Souper Saturday.

Mirela joined me in front of Tin Pan Alley, her breath visible in the frosty air. "Cold, is it not, sunshine?"

"It is." I had woolen gloves on and still had my hands jammed deep into my pockets. "Where's Guy?" As far as I'd been able to ascertain, when they weren't working, these two had been inseparable since the Lighting of the Monument. I wasn't sure what to make of it, but she seemed happy and was putting out canvas after canvas, probably overwhelming the guy in town who does her framing. She was on one hell of a creative streak, so that was something good. "Any news on the pirate-ship front?"

"It is important work," she said. She sounded a little defensive.

"I never said it wasn't," I said, puzzled. "I'm all for it. I think it's fascinating. And it's contributing something important to the world."

"We should be more like the pirates were," said Mirela with vehemence. She sounded positively fierce. "Our culture would be a better one."

"With no women?"

She shrugged. "So not perfect," she said. "But in many ways, they were better than us. And Guy thinks the more we know about them, perhaps the more we can learn from them."

I knew some of this. I've been to both Whydah museums. I'd looked it all up online. I knew the crews were multiethnic. I knew everyone on board was an equal shareholder in the ship's accounts. I even knew the quartermaster led the boarding parties, though I had no idea why I remembered that particular bit of obscure knowledge. And she was right: there was something to be said for the life. At least as far as Sam

Bellamy's ships went, they were as close as you could get to the Robin Hood of the high seas.

Still, it was odd hearing Mirela talk about it. As far as I knew, she'd never shown any interest in anything that didn't have to do with art or nature. Maybe it was love, after all.

I was stamping my feet with the cold by now, glaring up at Town Hall to see if I could see the clock. "Are they ever going to let us in?"

Mirela's text message sound went off, and she pulled her phone from her pocket. She stared at the screen for a very long moment, and then looked up at me, her face completely blank.

"What is it?" I asked. "Mirela! What's happened?"

"He has done it," she said, her voice curiously flat. "Guy has found it."

My eyes widened. "He's found the Mignonette?"

"No," she said. "The Bessie G. He has found the Bessie G."

***

"This is none of your business," said Julie Agassi.

I was trying to think of ways it could be. "I was the one who found Pete," I said.

She looked at me sharply. "You're kidding, right? *That's* the best you can do?"

I shrugged. We were standing at the end of MacMillan Pier, a cluster of people hanging out beside the really big boat—not exactly a nautical term, but I don't know anything about this stuff—tied up at the end, where the tall ships were when they came for the regatta, the biggest boat slip on the pier. Guy's Really Big Boat. Or one of them, anyway; according to Mirela, he had three out there, all of them towing proton precision magnetometers across the area he believed marked the wreck site of the Mignonette. In December. Something had made him accelerate his plans for sure.

I just didn't see how the Bessie G fit in. If she did.

In the meantime, the magnetometer, which didn't know it was just looking for pirate treasure, had picked up something else. In shallower water, Mirela told me, before someone from the Really Big Boat had come for her and brought her on board. *Sans* me. I wondered why they were looking outside of the area Guy had already selected. I wondered how the Really Big Boat managed in shallower water. I wondered a lot of things. I remembered saying something to him at the Lighting of the Monument—had that really only been a couple of weeks ago?—about a wreck also being a grave, and I shivered.

Julie had already been on board, had met with Roger the harbormaster, and Guy, and a whole bunch of other serious-looking people I didn't know. Now she was on the pier, frowning, as she finished speaking to the chief of police. "Send someone to talk to Helen," she said. "She has a right to be aware of what they're doing."

"So what is it?" I asked her. "What are they doing?"

Julie transferred the frown to me. "Are you still here?" She sighed. "He wants to raise it," she said.

I was a little shocked. "Can he do that?" I asked. "I mean, it's not his boat."

"Neither is that pirate ship he's after," Julie said. "Apparently if he wants to finance it, and insure it, and get all the other paperwork done and pay through the nose, he can. That seems to be the consensus."

"The question is, why?"

She looked at me sharply. "What do you mean?"

"Why would he want to?" I asked. "It's nothing to do with him."

"There's a lot of that going around," she said meaningfully.

I ignored her. "You just said it's expensive. And he has backers, people who expect him to be bringing up a pirate ship, not a fishing boat. So why's he taking the risk? What's in it for him?"

"And, I repeat, what does it have to do with you?"

I shrugged. "Sheer roaring curiosity," I said cheerfully. "Was that disarming enough for you to talk to me?"

"You're not nearly as cute as you think you are," said Julie. "And I have to go."

I was starting to feel like I was living in a pinball machine, rocketing from one bright shiny light to another, bouncing around frenetically until I came back to where I'd started. It was true I didn't have any personal reasons to be interested in what was happening—but there's something about being part of a community, too. For better or for worse, these were my people. The family I'd chosen over the one nature had saddled me with.

What I didn't want to do was stand out on the pier gawping like the tourists who'd come to town for Holly Folly and were now taking pictures, speculating among themselves as to what was going on. That something was going on, was clear: the air was fizzing with it, waves of questions and speculation and curiosity buffeting us.

Enough was enough. I left and headed down Commercial Street. It was one of those achingly clear and sharp winter days, when the air feels so cold and tight you could cut it with a knife, and the sky is an impossible blue. November's unexpected snowfalls had turned to slush and then melted altogether, and December was—so far—dry; otherwise we'd have looked like pages torn from a calendar. There wasn't any wind, which is really unusual for the Cape and for which I was grateful: the cold was—well, cold enough.

I think I ended up at the Race Point Inn because I didn't know where else to go. It's been my home away from home for so long, a space where I feel comfortable and competent, that it just seemed right.

Glenn couldn't sell it. He just couldn't.

The place was bustling; you'd never know it was the off-season. Some guests were sitting in the front lounge chatting over cookies and hot cider. One of the new guys, Luke, was behind the registration desk—the Race Point always seems to employ very young, very attractive men, which might have something to do with why the place was always busy. Eye candy for sure.

Glenn was drinking coffee in the lounge off the dining-room. I looked in, saw him, considered not going in, and then took a deep breath and changed my mind. If I started avoiding him now, it might never end. "Hey, Glenn."

He pulled his attention back from the middle distance where he'd been gazing and focused on me. "Sydney."

I gestured to the big velvet armchair next to his. "May I?"

"Sure, of course. You want some coffee?"

"No, I'm good." I began the long process of unwinding my wool muffler, putting gloves in pockets, finding a place to put my coat.

Glenn said, "Today's Barry's birthday."

I looked at him, startled. Every year during Bear Week I mark the day Barry died, but I'd completely spaced on his birthday, if in fact I'd ever known when it was. I sometimes forget my own birthday, much less anybody else's. I'm not the most organized person when it comes to stuff like that. I sat down and touched the back of his hand, lightly. "I'm so sorry," I said.

He smiled, but I couldn't see anything happy in his expression. "Sometimes I think he's going to walk in the door," he said. "And sometimes I can't remember what his voice sounded like."

Glenn hasn't gotten involved with anyone else since Barry's death, though Lord knows he's had plenty of opportunities. I wondered, briefly, if bears mate for life. The ones in the wild, I mean. "I miss him, too," I said, feeling the weight of the words' inadequacy.

He was still looking a little dazed. "I always used to come to town for Holly Folly," he said. "Back in the old days, you remember? He used to say how nice it was, Provincetown celebrating his birthday like this. He used to make that special punch, do you remember it? Fucking fantastic. Wouldn't let anyone know what was in it. He said it was his own secret recipe."

"I remember," I said.

Glenn nodded. "Great punch," he said. "He wouldn't even tell *me* what was in it, you know that? Not even me. Use to tease me about it no end. I could have everything of his, he'd say, but not that punch recipe. Kept it like some sort of state secret. His grandmother's favorite concoction, something like that." He paused. "You know, Sydney, I didn't ever imagine I'd be here without him."

"I know." It had taken me a while to feel comfortable with the inn without Barry in it, too. He haunted it, not in a scary sense, just in the expanse of his presence, his big enveloping presence. It had taken time for the echoes to recede, for the largeness of him to disappear altogether. I'm lying; of course it hadn't disappeared. Barry was still there in everything we planned, or thought about, or did.

Glenn shook his head, as if freeing it from something, scattering the cobwebs of his thoughts. "We should talk business," he said. "Adrienne's dinner is tomorrow night."

I nodded. "Sold out," I said. Every Holly Folly, Adrienne, our diva chef, does a special holiday dinner. It's very expensive, very exclusive, and tickets for it sell out in October. One seating only. Dishes that people talk about for months. We have a string quartet from the Cape Symphony Orchestra that plays during the dinner, and there's a silent auction that benefits the AIDS Support Group.

This is one event at the Race Point I don't organize: it's Mike and the maître d's special moment. Together with Adrienne the diva chef, they plan for it all year. The restaurant is decorated with fresh branches and boughs so the room smells like a pine forest. There's a tremendous Christmas tree in one corner, rivalling the one in the front lounge and the even bigger one outside the front door, and fairy lights sparkling everywhere, berries and red bows. And that's before I even begin to talk about the wines, and the food… "It's going to be fabulous," I said. It is, every year. Another of Barry's traditions.

Glenn was thinking along the same lines. "The inn looks perfect. He'd love Holly Folly this year," he said, looking around the room.

"He loved Holly Folly every year," I said.

He straightened then, as if snapping himself out of the gloom. "What weddings do you have coming up?" he asked.

I went with the shift of topic. "Erin and Charles on Wednesday," I said. I always stick with first names for my couples, which I gather is fairly unusual in the world of wedding planning where everything seems to be a step removed from actual human contact, but it works for me. "That's here. And then there's nothing until Christmas Eve, Stephen and Carl. They want to do it outside if it's not actually stormy."

Glenn shrugged. "Fifty-fifty chance," he said.

"Or worse," I agreed. "Someone contacted me about something informal for the day after Christmas, but I'm waiting to hear. And there are two weddings on New Year's."

"Guests?"

"To the weddings? Nothing over ten people." Weddings in P'town are informal at the best of times, and winter weather discourages travel and outdoor extravaganzas. Besides, come the new year, there's not much for out-of-town guests to actually *do* once they're here. In January, you can walk down Commercial Street at seven in the evening and be the only person out. Not many people find that attractive in a vacation destination.

"Okay, good. We need to talk about New Year's Eve," he said. That was fine. We keep it fairly low-key at the inn—there's a fancy-dress ball at town hall, most people who want to go out, go to that—but we always organize a bit of a soirée for guests who happen to be at the inn, with someone playing the grand piano in the restaurant and a countdown with champagne. The next day, we make watching the parade on television a brunch affair, mimosas and Bloody Marys while we put the Rose Bowl floats on the big-screen in the dining room.

"Sure. I think we're all set. What still needs to be settled?"

He seemed to be about to say something when the front door opened and wind gusted into the reception area and, with it, somewhat to my surprise, Guy and Mirela. She spotted me straightaway and took his arm to steer him our way. "Sydney! So many people in town!"

"A lot going on," I said. I was still adapting to thinking about and seeing Mirela as part of a couple.

Guy was sliding out of his muffler and coat. "That wind!" he exclaimed, then looked around him. "Can we get a bottle of champagne?" he asked Glenn. "Four glasses, of course."

"Of course," Glenn echoed. He turned and called out to Luke. "Get Sam to bring up a bottle of Veuve Cliquot." He obviously already knew Guy's taste and budget.

Guy and Mirela arranged themselves on the settee across from us. I was a little startled at how—bright—she looked, if that word makes any sense. She was sparkling like the champagne, like sun on crisp white snow, picking out each individual crystal. I'd never seen Mirela in love, I realized. This was different from the occasional boyfriends (and even girlfriends) I'd seen her with: them, she picked up and discarded like dubious spring fashions. This was Mirela looking *happy*.

Guy seemed in high spirits as well. He fussed a little over helping Mirela out of her coat and for a moment I had a sudden vision of them in thirty years, him still fussing over her and her telling him not to, their hair gray, their faces lined. I blinked and the image dissolved and disappeared, and the inn reclaimed its clear sharp lines and colors around us.

Sam—another of the handsome young men Mike likes to hire—appeared with the champagne and made a show of arranging the glasses and the ice bucket. "Shall I open it?" he asked, his smile dazzling. I wondered what that smile made him in tips. Probably enough to retire on.

"Splendid," Guy said. "No, Sam, thank you, I'll take care of it." And he did, with elegance. I had a feeling that Guy did everything with elegance. He poured as expertly as any sommelier, put the bottle down and then raised his glass, looking at us expectantly.

"What are we drinking to?" I asked. Not that I cared: any opportunity to drink Veuve Cliquot is a great opportunity.

"To Guy," said Mirela, looking at him, her eyes as sparkling as the bubbles in her glass.

He was smiling broadly as he looked from her to us. He stood up, took her hand in his free one and kissed it. "I have news," he said, slowly and portentously. "Tomorrow," he paused, to give the announcement its full effect, "we're raising the Bessie G."

There was a moment, just a second really, of silence, and then, from the arched doorway where no one had seen him come in, Mike said, "*And* they're reopening the investigation into Tony Correia's murder."

That's a lot for just one glass of champagne.

13

And, just like that, the town changed.

Which isn't to say that Holly Folly was impacted; it's going to take more than an old murder and a new salvage operation to do that. People plan for this all year; but now it seemed revelers had more to do than just stroll the streets, make Christmas purchases, and party.

This Holly Folly, it seemed, it was all about corpses.

Pete started it, though information about his death was still pretty much under wraps, so there wasn't any news; the district attorney kept telling the press that it was an ongoing investigation and that conclusions would be released once they were drawn, and everyone who checked the Cape Cod Times and the Province-town Banner for updates was disappointed. With the number of overdoses on the Cape so alarmingly on the increase, the consensus seemed to be that Pete had done it himself and nobody had been around with Narcan when he did. Still, no matter how it happens, there's an unmistakable frisson that runs through a small community when someone dies, and the tourists just added a layer of horrified fascination to the mix.

But Pete's death hadn't started it, not really; it had started five years ago, when someone shot Tony Correia out in the East End—and why was he out there?—and the Bessie G had disappeared into the night. And there was something in the air this Holly Folly, something both exciting and frightening, as we seemed to be moving toward a resolution of sorts, though no one knew exactly what was going to be resolved or if resolution was even what anybody wanted. I know I was feeling unsettled by the whole thing—well, especially about Pete, but I took that a little personally; finding a dead body will do that for you—but I could sense that others were, too.

The fishing community, smaller now than it had ever been, did whatever is the twenty-first-century equivalent of pulling up the drawbridge and getting ready to defend the castle. This was one of their own, a family just like theirs, and now a bright spotlight was pointing their way.

And that's why I was surprised as hell when Helen Correia called me.

I'd gone home, cranky and wondering if the scratchiness I was feeling all over was the beginnings of a flu. I didn't recognize the number on the display and almost let it go to voicemail. Almost. At some point, I was hoping, Ali was going to call me, and who knew what phone he might need to use? That was one call I didn't want to miss.

"Is that Sydney Riley?"

"Yes," I said. There was a longish pause, and I said, louder and encouragingly, "This is Sydney Riley."

"Um… hi. You don't know me, Miss Riley. My name is Helen Correia. You've probably heard…" Her voice trailed off; she didn't want to rehash any of this. She sounded exhausted. That wasn't altogether surprising.

"I know who you are," I said, trying to get as much warmth into my voice as I could. "What can I do for you, Ms. Correia?"

"Oh, call me Helen, please… I just thought…" A pause and I could almost feel her taking hold of herself. I could hear her swallow. "I'm sorry. I don't mean to take up your time like this. It's just that people say that you're something like a detective," she said.

Oh, great. When I wasn't the town's Jessica Fletcher, I was Miss Marple. And the truth was, they were both eons smarter than me. "Ms. Correia—Helen—I'm really not. I don't have any official standing." What do I say: I've been at the right place at the right time for murder? One could argue about what "right" meant in that context. And not to mention that I "solved" cases by blundering around until the answer hit me over the head, occasionally literally.

She hesitated. "Oh. Well. Yes, I understand that." She seemed to be trying to pull herself together. "The reason I'm calling you is, I knew Emilia Mattos," she said, seemingly irrelevantly.

Mrs. Mattos! I was smiling just hearing her name. My longtime neighbor; at some point, I liked to think, perhaps even my friend. Some days it felt as if she'd been gone forever; some days I still expected to look out my front window and see her sweeping out her front steps, her hair tied back into a severe bun, an apron over her clothing. Her house had remained empty since her death: there was some protracted legal battle going on. Provincetown real estate is ridiculously expensive, and someone was someday going to make a lot of money from it. "She thought very highly of you, don't you know," Helen Correia was saying.

"I thought highly of her, too," I said softly.

"I see." She was struggling but, I thought, brave to have even gotten this far with me. "She told me once you had helped her. She said that talking to you, it wasn't like talking to the police, not at all the same. She said that you understood... *us*, you know, the townspeople. What we're like. What's important to us."

Only washashores use the term "townie."

Helen was still talking. "She said you'd become very dear to her, and well, I trusted her, don't you know. I'd known her since I was born, practically. Whatever she said, I believed. And we knew each other, you see, from so long ago, so I thought maybe since she trusted you, I could trust you, too… I'm sorry," she said finally. "I'm not saying any of this right. I'd just like to talk to someone who isn't the police. And I know I can trust you to help, because you helped her."

There was a definite lump in my throat now. I remembered, suddenly, that amazing kale soup. "I'll do what I can," I said. "I'm honestly not sure how much help I can be, though. What is it, exactly, that…?" I had a good feeling I already knew, but I wasn't about to put words into her mouth.

"You know about my brother," she said cautiously, and then, before I could answer, she burst out, "I know you know. Everyone knows about it. It's out in the public. They're bringing up his boat, don't you know, and I don't see how I can stand it." She took a beat, no more, to get hold of herself. "The truth is, Miss Riley, I don't know what's going to be there, and I want to know, while at the same time, I don't want to know, and on top of it all I'm a little afraid…"

I took a deep breath, my go-to action when I don't know what to say or do. I didn't know if Guy had her permission to raise the Bessie G; I didn't even know if he *needed* her permission to raise the Bessie G. Some mysterious maritime law applied, no doubt. Not my business. "Are you planning on being there when they bring the boat in?" I asked. I had no idea even if I was using the correct terminology. Raise it? Float it? Winch it? In a way, in a different way, I was as adrift here as Helen.

There was something like a sob on the other end of the phone. "I'm not married," she said, seemingly out of nowhere.

"No," I agreed cautiously.

"So it's not as if I had a husband, don't you know, someone to lean on, and I'm not used to—oh, I'm not saying this right. I'm not looking for anyone to make my decisions for me, it's just I don't want to be alone in… well, making them, and *presenting* them, to other people, don't you know."

I took another breath. "Helen, I'll be happy to support you in whatever you want. I'll tell you what. Why don't I come and pick you up tomorrow, and take you to the harbor when—when they bring it in? We can go together. I'll stay as long as you need me." The gallery, I thought, would have to survive my absence, which was unfortunate as we headed into Holly Folly, but that was life.

There was a pause. "Yes," she said, doubtfully. "Yes, that would be fine. I mean to say, that's very kind of you. Thank you. But you have to know: there's more. I mean, there are some things you should know before tomorrow. Before it happens. But it's nothin' I want to talk to the police about. I don't want to tell the police." A pause. "You have to understand. I don't trust the police."

There was a story there, somewhere, but it seemed a low priority in the layers of stories I was getting. She might or might not tell me; but in any case it wasn't the story currently on offer. And if she was anything like Mrs. Mattos, there would be no budging her, either. "Do you want to tell *me*?" I asked.

"I have to tell *someone*," she said. Okay, ego deflator. At least I qualified as someone. "It's just that…"

I took another breath, eyeing Ibsen who was doing his special copyrighted Cute Thing and trying to entice me to come and scratch him under the chin and give him treats. I had to just accept the inevitable: I was definitely *not* in for the night. "Helen, do you want to talk to me now? Tonight, I mean? I can meet you somewhere if you want." Desperately running through the options, which were few and far between: most places open for Holly Folly were going to be filled with revelers. Not conducive to a private tête-à-tête. "I don't know where you live, but we can meet at Far Land," I said tentatively. It wasn't perfect, but I wasn't seeing other options. The Canteen, one of my personal go-to meeting places, was running its annual fabulously popular Holiday Winter Market. Way too much going on *there*.

There was a long pause as she thought it over. Far Land Provisions is one of the most mixed-media, so to speak, places in town. It's casual and convenient and you can get a snack or a coffee and sit for a while; the pastries are amazing, and there's free wi-fi. Everyone goes there: visitors, townies, old Portuguese residents, gay and straight and everything in between. It was the best I could offer on the spur of the moment.

I could feel her balancing it, visualizing the tables and their proximity to each other, thinking about the music and the people, making a decision. "You could come here," she said at length, cautiously. "To my house, I mean. I live alone."

"Okay," I said. "That's fine, too." So she didn't want to go public, even in the neutral territory of Far Land. This wasn't just a secret, it was a serious one. I pulled a notebook toward me and scowled at the list on the top page that I hadn't even begun to tackle. "Where do you live?"

"On Court Street." She gave me the address. "I don't mean to get you out on a night like this," she added. "It's very good of you, don't you know, and I feel badly, I do, it's just—"

"I know," I said reassuringly. "It's fine, it's okay, really." I'd been looking forward to a quiet night—down on Commercial Street, they were doing Drag Bingo tonight, Holly Folly in full-throat celebration, I generally stayed away from that—but there was something in Helen's voice.

And Court Street was hardly Holly Folly territory.

Besides that, everyone who kept saying it was actually right: I did like a mystery. Sad, but true.

"Give me twenty minutes," I said. I am such a sucker.

Ibsen had given up on a cuddle and was looking hopefully at his bowl, making the little sounds that pass in his world for meowing; I never figured out why he can't meow like every other cat. Then again, I've never figured why he can't bury his poop in the litter box like every other cat. "I'm going out again," I announced.

He was unimpressed. He looked pointedly at the bowl. I gave in. This is why I've never had children; I'm no stickler for discipline. They'd be running amuck inside five minutes. I opened a can and put half of it in a dish and made sure he had water to go with it. "You'll be okay on your own for a while?"

He didn't answer. He never does.

Put the coat, gloves, scarf, and hat back on. One day I'm moving someplace where I don't need to have completely different wardrobes in order to get through a year. (I say that every winter here, but the truth is, what would I do if I didn't have the winter to complain about?)

Court Street is a short walk from where I live, and I had a sense that Helen didn't particularly want the Little Green Car parked in her driveway, so I walked. Everyone knows everyone else's vehicles in this town. I nearly froze on the way over—the wind had picked up again, it was going to be One of Those Nights—but I made it before frostbite had quite set in.

Helen's apartment felt overheated after the cold, and the first thing I noticed was that if there was a surface in there without knick-knacks on it, I wasn't seeing it. She had ceramic sad-eyed puppies and vases holding plastic flowers; ashtrays and bowls overflowing with shells; jars filled with sea glass, old Sandwich glass doo-dads scattered everywhere. Photos propped up on every surface, some in frames, some without: old faces, carefree faces, serious faces. Pictures of fishing-boats, houses, people on the beach. A whole life, a whole family un-folding around me, birthdays and christenings and Christmases, joys and sorrows all in a diz-zying array in one room, seasons swirling around us at telescopic speed. You could stand there and read the town's whole history, if you had the time.

Helen herself was plucking nervously at the edges of the apron she was wearing, somewhat oddly, over her jeans and sweater. Tonight her hair was pulled back into a ponytail, brown with streaks of gray in it, her eyes alight with some-thing I couldn't recognize. "I'll take your coat," she said, practically pulling it off me. "There's port. Will you have a glass of port?"

"Um, thanks, yes, thank you." Whatever she wanted: this was her gig. The coat and Helen both disappeared into a back room. "Sit down," she called. "I won't be a minute."

The furniture had to have been inherited, I thought; it was heavy, imposing, meant for a larger room than the one it was in now, and I imagined a family house enclosing all everything here, Helen's mother ironing the antimacassars, her father filling a pipe in one of the worn recliners, life happening before they had to sell it. Helen had probably moved into a spinster aunt's house, moving gently and inevitably into the role of spinster herself.

I found I was sitting on the very edge of the sofa—one not unlike my own, that seems to swallow anyone who dared to lean back—and feeling a little overwhelmed. There was so much stuff here, it was almost suffocating. I wonder how anyone lived in the midst of it.

I wondered what it said about the person who could live in the midst of it.

Helen had mysteriously moved from bedroom to kitchen while I was taking stock, and now she emerged from the kitchen, minus the apron, holding two small glasses in one hand and carrying a decanter in the other. "Here we are," she said, unnecessarily, putting everything down on the coffee table, which had no fewer than four lace doilies on it already; she positioned everything she was carrying carefully on top of them. "I thought I had some cake," she said, her eyes traveling distractedly from my face to the decanter to the doorway into the kitchen, "but I think I don't."

"That's fine," I said. "I'm not hungry."

"Still," she said doubtfully. "I ought to offer you *something*."

"I'm looking forward to the port," I said truthfully if hesitatingly. There's port and there's port. "Please don't trouble yourself further."

She sat, as I did, on the edge of her chair and poured the port with care, making sure that both glasses had exactly the same amount of liquid in them. She stoppered the decanter, picked up a glass, and passed it across to me with a certain level of ceremony. I took it and waited. I wasn't sure exactly what her ceremony entailed but damned if I was going to make the first move.

Helen took a tentative sip, as though reticent about the wickedness of it all, and I did the same. The port was surprisingly good, deep and mellow and rich, spreading inside with a slow glow of warmth.

She looked around the room as though searching for inspiration and finally her eyes came back to me. "I've lived in this house my whole life," she said.

"It feels comfortable," I said. "Is there a photo here of your brother?" It was a good bet: the number of photographs she had scattered around that room, she probably had the whole genealogy.

Helen picked up a framed photo from the table at her elbow; it was a fluid gesture, and I had a feeling she'd been sitting there for a long time, perhaps even for years, picking up that photograph and studying it. Wondering, perhaps, how things had come to such a pass that he'd ended up with a bullet in his skull. "Yes. Here's Tony," she said, and passed it across.

It was taken on a sunny day, a summer day, you could feel the heat rising off the image, could almost taste the salt and sun on your tongue, smell the sunscreen lotion, hear the gulls. He was standing on the deck of a boat—presumably the Bessie G—in a sleeveless shirt and holding up a fish. Something big; I didn't know any more about fish than I did about boats. But he was clearly pleased with it; he was laughing, his head tipped back and eyes filled with something warm and happy.

It took me a moment to hand the photo back. I didn't want to let go of the moment.

Helen had put down her glass and took the frame into her lap, holding it with both hands, like a book. She trailed her fingertips over the image, as I thought she probably had hundreds of times before, regret tainting the memory. "He was my little brother," she said softly, then looked up at me. "I mostly raised him, don't you know. Our mother died of the cancer when he was little, and Dad was out with the fleet, so it was just Tony and me. He was more like my son than my brother." So the ghosts I'd imagined, her parents growing old together in another house, had been someone else's ghosts entirely. Helen's eyes were bright with tears. "I'll be honest with you: I thought I'd die, too, when they found him, don't you know."

"And you have no idea who would want to kill him?" The words were out of my mouth before I thought about them. *Very smooth and subtle, Riley.*

Helen didn't seem to mind. She shook her head. "Who'd want to shoot someone like that?" she asked rhetorically. "No money, he didn't have nothin' to steal. Didn't do nothin' to nobody. My Tony." She took a deep, shuddering breath, her fingers still on the glass, as through reading it as braille, as though drawing strength from it. "I saw him," she said suddenly, her voice hardening, shaping itself into something serious and not at all nostalgic.

I took another sip of port; I had a feeling I was going to need it. I tried to put on an encouraging expression. "I'm sorry. Who did you see?"

"Tony. I saw him when he set out, that night."

This was news. I set down my glass, carefully, on the lace doily closest to me. I didn't want to spook her any more than she already was. "You saw Tony the night the boat disappeared, you mean?" I asked carefully. "Do you mean—*in* the boat?"

She nodded. "I was down the pier," she said. "I'd come down to see him. He didn't go out much at night, as a rule, don't you know, but I'd seen Sarah down to the A&P market, and she said he was going out that night. An' it wasn't that out of the ordinary, not really, when I come to think of it. I didn't imagine nothin' being wrong." She paused and took a breath, measuring out her words, measuring out her emotions. "So I went ahead and made him some soup—she was busy with the girls, no need for her to bother." I had a vivid flash of what it had been like for him, with two women in his life vying to take care of him. "So I brought soup down the pier. I knew he was going out, and I'd made some soup." She shook her head. "Sarah, now, she was good to him, I won't say any different, but she had the girls, don't you know. And once a woman has children, they're the ones she looks after, not her man. But Tony, he was my child, like I said. So I brought him soup."

I dampened my lips and tried to dampen my enthusiasm at the same time. "Tell me what you saw," I said. She was dying to, anyway.

She kept one hand on the photograph and reached the other out, a little blindly, for her glass, downing the rest of the port in one great swallow. "Tony wouldn't let me come on board," she said. "That's what's stayed with me, don't you know. He always had me on board, from when he first bought that boat off of Joe

Santis, and so proud he was that day. Always proud of the Bessie G." She took a shuddering breath. "So I brought him the soup and I was going to go and put it in the wheelhouse, like I always did, and he said no, Helen, never mind that, I'm casting off."

She looked at her glass, registered it was empty, and shook her head. "I said, Tony, that's nothin' can't wait for a few minutes, I'll get you all squared away in no time at all, and he raised his voice to me. Never in our whole lives did Tony raise his voice to me, don't you know." Her eyes sought mine, looking for understanding. I nodded, and she seemed to take encouragement from it. "He said no, Helen, go on home with you. He took that soup from my hand without a thank-you, without nothin', just anxious to be away, and he didn't even look me in the eyes. Nothin' like I was used to. I couldn't figure it out."

There was a pause; she swallowed a couple of times. I finally asked, as gently as I could, "Do you think there was someone else on board?" I didn't know exactly what the wheelhouse comprised or whether there was space anywhere for anyone to be hidden. I really needed to learn more about boats if I was going to continue to live at the seaside. "Is there any place someone else could be hidden?"

She looked at me as though I'd lost my mind. "Down below," she said. "But why? Why would anybody be there?"

"It might explain why Tony didn't want to get you involved," I said. "If there were somebody there, someone threatening him, he might have wanted to keep you safe."

She was staring at me now. "You mean the person who killed him? They coulda been there all that time?"

I shrugged. "It's possible," I said uncomfortably. "Helen, this is something the police really should—"

She cut me off. "Not talking to the police," she said, waving the idea away with her hand. "I thought someone should know, is all. Someone should know he wasn't quite right when he set out. But I'm not telling tales to the likes of the police."

I tried another tack. "Do you think that maybe Sarah and the girls could have been on board as well?" I asked. "Maybe that's another reason he wanted you to stay off the boat. Maybe he was protecting all of you." But from whom? You just had to keep circling back to that question: who would want an ordinary fisherman killed?

Unless he wasn't an ordinary fisherman.

Helen was looking at me blankly, and I floundered a little getting back to the conversation. "Did the police ask you about this back—when it happened?" I asked.

She got up, fetched the decanter, refilled our glasses. "Bother you if I smoke?" she asked. "Funny, you have to ask, these days."

I shook my head. "That's fine." It wasn't, really; it would take me two washings to get the smell out of my hair; but it was her house and her story. And now that I had a semi-official presence in the midst of it, I wasn't going to do anything that would put her off.

Helen lit her cigarette and I waited through the first inhale and exhale. "There," she said, as if satisfied. She looked at me finally. "They asked," she said. "The police. They asked when I'd seen him last. Asked me if anything had seemed funny about him. I wasn't going to tell them. I didn't want to get Tony in no trouble."

Now we were getting somewhere. "Because he would have been?" I asked. "What was Tony doing?" And, as she looked like she was about to shut down again, I added, "Helen, you're the one who asked me here, you're the one who wants me to help. I can't help unless you tell me the truth. *All* the truth." I added hurriedly. "Everything that happened. I'm not judging anybody." Hell, she should know that, Province-town's the least judgmental place on earth. "Just tell me."

She puffed on the cigarette for a moment, then took a hefty swallow of port before clearing her throat. "I don't know nothin' for sure," she said. "That's the problem, don't you know. That I don't know how to put it all together." She glanced at me, and my impatience must have been showing, for she went back to staring at the worn carpet as she spoke. "Tony went out that night," she said. "An' he went out some other nights, too. An' that's what was new. He never used to go out at night. Sure, a lot of them do, you has to go out farther these days for anything, an' in winter there's not much daylight to be had anyway. And them fish, they don't know if it's day or night. But Sarah, she used to be way strict about it all, she'd say she wanted him home at night. Very old-fashioned, Sarah was."

I stopped myself from looking around the room, which easily could have come out of anyone's grandmother's place. If Helen was calling Sarah old-fashioned, she must have been talking about another century altogether. "So that night he was—killed, that wasn't the first time you'd seen him go out at night?"

She shook her head. "An' I was gearing up to ask him about it, don't you know," she said. "Only we didn't see that much of each other, not to talk to. Sure, maybe after Mass at St. Pete's, but Sarah an' the girls'd be there, an' I thought it would be better to do it alone. But I never got the chance, 'cause that was the last night I seen him."

"How many times did you see him before that?" I asked. "Going out at night, I mean?" Because that was the one bit of information that the police might have been able to do something with. Julie Agassi had taught me that: a change in any pattern is meaningful. If the person never went to the movies on a weeknight and then abruptly started going on a Tuesday, it was significant. If someone always did their laundry on a Saturday and hadn't shown up at the laundromat for two successive Saturdays, it was significant. The significance might be minor—the person might have started taking a weekend class that kept them from the laundromat, or found someone to date who liked going to the movies on Tuesdays—but it remained significant. People don't change established patterns of behavior without a reason.

If Sarah had wanted Tony at home in the evenings so badly that it dictated how he managed his workload, then his stepping out of that pattern had to mean something. First, because it's hard to break a behavior—ask anyone who's tried to stop smoking or start exercising. And, second, because breaking this particular pattern came with unwanted consequences at home. That added up to Something Significant for sure.

Helen didn't have to give it much thought; she had a small spiral-bound notebook to hand. "Usually I just write my shopping lists in here," she said, putting her cigarette in the ashtray and flipping through the pages. "But sometimes… okay, here it is." She looked up at me. "Seven times in the two months," she said. "That I *seen*, don't you know. There coulda been others."

"And that's a lot?" I was feeling mildly deflated; seven oddly scheduled trips over two months didn't seem to add up to anything. I'd been anticipating maybe one or two a week.

"For Tony?" She was staring at me. "You didn't know him. Regular as clockwork, that man, don't you know."

I took a deep breath. I was supposed to be some kind of detective; it was time I started detecting something here. "What did Sarah think was going on?" I asked. She was the one who would really know. Unfortunately, she was unavailable for interviews.

Helen shook her head. "Din't talk to her about it," she said. "She wouldna've told me, anyways. Even though I'm family, that was something she would've kept just between her and Tony. Old-school, that was Sarah, don't you know."

I hid a quick smile at Helen calling someone else old-school. But behind it all, an image was emerging: for all that Sarah had been young when she disappeared—probably only a few years older than me—she was clearly Province-town Portuguese down to her toes. That meant something. It meant a spotless house, a strict work ethic, and a strong belief in the healing properties of kale soup. And something more, something that defied definition, a backbone, an inner strength, a faith in the power of the Rosary and the saints in heaven to get you through life's problems—with the sure knowledge that you had to pull your own weight, too.

Time to try another tack. "Okay," I said. "But since Tony died, and the boat disappeared, you must have thought about it a lot, about those extra night trips." Thought about it a lot? Good one, Riley. Helen would have defined herself through her family; thinking about her brother's untoward death had probably been front-of-mind for her for eight years. She woke with it, she lived her day with it, she went to bed with it.

Helen was considering the question. "At first I thought he was fishing illegally," she said. "Them guys from New Bedford, the big fleet, they come here and do scalloping right on the shoreline up to Herring Cove, don't you know. Plenty illegal fishing goin' on. The fisheries are just too strict for someone wants to make a decent living." She glanced up at me, a quick look to see how I was taking her laissez-faire attitude about quotas. I kept my face blank. The truth is, I have mixed feelings about the whole fisheries thing. I absolutely understand that everything's been over-fished—the fish that gave Cape Cod its name can hardly be found around here anymore—and that stocks need to replenish; and I understand there are people who have no other options for making a living, whose entire fortune is in their boat, and cutting off their fish is cutting off a lifeline.

It's not people like Tony Correia who got us here, of course; it's the big factory fleets that really sucked the fish from the sea. But the Tony

184

Correias, the smaller fleets, they're the ones who have to pay the price. And so, yeah, sometimes the rules are broken.

I said, "Helen, if Tony was fishing something he shouldn't have been, that's none of my business. I just want to help you here."

She stubbed out the end of the cigarette. "I don't know it for sure," she said. "You just asked me what I thought he might be doing, an' that's what I thought, that's what I've thought all this time. He had a mortgage on that Bessie G. He had two girls he had to take care of. Sarah worked, sure, but sellin' fried clams down to John's Footlong in the season an' unemployment in the winter, that only gets you so far. They needed Tony to bring in the money, an' it was getting' harder and harder for him, for all of 'em. So that's what I thought." She said it firmly, almost fiercely, as though challenging me to contradict her.

I wasn't about to. She was probably right. "I won't tell the police about this right now," I said. "But the time may come when we have to. I won't talk about it without talking to you first."

"I just want you to find out what happened to him," she said.

"I know." I was feeling woefully inadequate to the task. "Tomorrow…" I let my voice trail off, waiting to see where she was with the whole bringing the Bessie G up thing.

"Tomorrow we'll know," she said. "Funny thing. I was all resentful of that man—what's his name? Funny name."

"Guy Husband," I said.

She nodded. "Him. Outsider, don't know nothin' about us or who we are or what we care about, he comes in with his money an' his scientific method an' all, an' I thought, who's this, to come an' intrude on something that's ours, don't you know."

"I know," I said. I'd been thinking along the same lines.

"But now he says he's got our boat," she said, and I could feel the tightness behind her voice as she spoke, "now that I know it's her, I'm glad he's here an' he's doin' it. Knowing something has to be better than not knowing nothin'." She paused. "I just don't get it, Sydney," she said, and I wondered why it was the first time she'd spoken my name. "He goes out at night, an' I saw him go out, I know my brother and I know the Bessie G, an' I know he went out that night. Then why did he come back without the boat? Why did someone shoot him out in East End? It don't make no sense to me."

"It doesn't make sense to anyone, I think," I said cautiously; but it was true that if anyone had had any brilliant ideas about it, they would have become common knowledge by now. "Maybe we'll know more tomorrow."

"Or maybe even less," she said darkly.

14

Mirela was losing her mind.

That was my first thought when I stopped by her studio the next morning. She doesn't usually paint during Holly Folly; she's a lot more likely to be out and about, selling her paintings, having meals and drinks and coffee with patrons—and she has quite a few of them—meeting new people, getting commissions, all that. It's her best time of year for sales, present and future, far better even than she does during the summer season. So I expect to see her in passing, in social situations, and that's about it.

But when I called her mobile, thinking she'd be at the Race Point Inn or possibly even out with Guy, she said she'd spent the night at her studio.

Which was decidedly weird. I couldn't remember the last time Mirela spent a night in her studio.

I finished off my second coffee and shrugged into my coat. Ibsen was looking askance at me and, as usual, the guilt thing worked; I left him with a pile of treats. He accepted it as his due and never gave me a backward glance. Ingrate.

The wind was gusting down Commercial Street, sharp and cutting with its cold, making me feel breathless with the frigid air I inhaled. Mirela's studio was, by contrast, ridiculously hot. As was Mirela herself, wearing a t-shirt and jeans with holes at the knees, her blonde hair pinned on top of her head without benefit of mirror or comb.

And she was *painting*. There were five or six unfinished canvases grouped around her while she worked on one propped on her main easel, a staggering number of works in progress, but the thing was, you could tell immediately that something was seriously wrong. When she first came to P'town, Mirela painted landscapes, peaceful sunsets over fishing boats at the pier, dune grasses and oceanscapes, even some street scenes. Over the past few years, her style evolved into something progressively more and more abstract, images in which the sails on the boats were hinting at rather than explained, the sparkle on the sea a matter of interpretation. Both styles were intimately, obviously Mirela, no matter how distinct they seemed from each other, expressionist or realist. These paintings were neither.

These paintings were about death.

I stood in the middle of the room in the wintry washed-out light from the big windows facing the harbor and felt like I'd been invited to a special episode of hell. There were people in the paintings, people drowning, people screaming, people dying. Mouths and eyes twisted in pain, hands grasping. Water rising up over their heads and the soundless screams echoing around the room. "Oh, my God, Mirela. What are you *doing*?"

She didn't turn around. "I could not sleep," she said. "There were these people in my head. I had to let them out."

"Who are they?"

"I do not know." She hadn't stopped dabbing maniacally at the canvas since I'd come in. The sheer energy this output had taken was astounding. And more than a little frightening. "It's the people on the Bessie G, isn't it?" I asked.

"I do not know," she said again.

It was; it had to be. Three distinct faces—it could only be the three missing women, Sarah Correia and her two daughters—drowning in dark waters. I shivered. Had something Guy said put the idea to Mirela? Or her own imagination, let loose on what she thought they'd find when they raised the fishing boat? Something she'd intuited without understanding rationally? Whatever it was, it was definitely creepy.

I'd never seen this level of frenzied energy in her before; it reminded me of the long-ago days when I'd dabbled in cocaine, the manic teeth-clenching nerve-burning high that resulted. I used mine to watch DVD after DVD for two days straight, which was pretty useless; but I knew people who had talent and did what Mirela was doing now, riding insane busts of creative energy that in the end produced stuff that wasn't nearly as beautiful as the drug suggested it would be. I didn't think for a moment Mirela was on coke, or anything else—she's really something of a prude, to tell the truth—but it certainly looked the same. Something manic was fraying her nerves, walking behind her and pushing her forward into something dark and out of control.

And I had no idea whether I should help her snap out of it, or just leave her to it. Was it a useful outlet, or was it going to damage her? I said the only thing I could think of. "Have you eaten anything recently?"

"I do not have time for that." She paused for so brief a moment I might have imagined it, whirled, and attacked one of the unfinished pieces with her brush, bright slashes of red across the pictures, blood seeping through its pores. The canvas was propped on a chair and the seat was already looking like a crime scene.

"Do you want me to bring you anything?" I was sounding like someone's mother. Not mine; mine would have already had me halfway to the asylum, always supposing there was one nearby. But someone's mother. The kind of mother who offers platitudes along with her chicken soup.

"No." I might as well have not even been in the room. This is the point at which my mother would have given an exaggerated sigh and left in a huff.

I just left. I was suddenly feeling incredibly, ineffably sad. Mirela was making images of death; Helen was worrying about her family; the Bessie G was being raised, the ghosts it sheltered calling out from the past; Ali was still MIA; Pete was dead; the future of the inn was up in the air; and my mother was still going to be coming for Christmas.

A jolly Holly Folly indeed.

***

You'd think with all that going on, my life couldn't get too much more complicated. You'd be wrong. This is me, after all, Sydney Riley, we're talking about. My life is never not complicated.

I wanted to be down at the pier when they brought the Bessie G in, but that wasn't going to be until the afternoon, as I found out when I called Craig. He seemed bemused to hear from me. "Hey, Sydney, I never see you, and now it's twice in two weeks!"

"You're not seeing me. We're on the telephone." I'd called the harbormaster's office; Craig had answered. Toss of the dice.

"Same difference. What's up, Sydney? How can I help you?"

"I wanted to ask a few questions about the Bessie G." Inspired, I added, "Don't worry, it's not just that I'm nosy. Helen Correia's asked me to—well, sort of represent her. Informally, that is, I mean. Um—maybe help her find out what happened. And at least help her have a look at it once it's raised. So I told her I'd call and see what I could find out." Dropping Helen's name wouldn't hurt; Craig's no washashore, he's old-time Provincetown himself, and the natives all know each other generations back. What he wouldn't necessarily do for me, he'd do for Helen.

"They're out there now," he said. "The marine salvage rig, the archaeologists, everyone. Got there way before first light, I hear."

Archaeologists for a missing fishing boat? "When are they coming in? Do you have any idea?"

"Roger says before it's dark. He's been on the radio with them. That guy with the funny name, Guy—"

"—Husband," I finished. I wondered why he'd never changed his name. This must happen to him every day of his life. Kids must have devastated him in the schoolyard.

"That's the one." A spate of conversation, away from the receiver, and then he came back. "Says the boat's intact."

"Ok—ay," I said, slowly, drawing the word out. "Um, Craig, I have no idea what that means. It's in good shape? What?"

Craig's a good guy. Anyone else would have told me to go look it up. He probably didn't even roll his eyes. Well, maybe just a little. "You know, the Whydah?" he asked rhetorically. "She was so hard to find, see, and they're still exploring her, years after Whittier found her? It's because the site's what they call exploded. An exploded site means the ship shattered when she went down, scattering stuff all over the seabed. Sometimes it can scatter for miles. But this is the opposite. The Bessie G didn't explode, that's why they can raise her. You're right, actually, she's in good shape, she still looks like a boat. Plus, she's in shallower water," he added, considering the issue. "That helps a lot too. Makes her easier to raise."

"I see." What I didn't see was how that helped me at all. "So—they're coming in this afternoon?"

"Yeah. They're on their way back, give it a couple of hours, you can bring Helen down to see her."

"Thanks, Craig." I clicked off the telephone and decided coffee would clear my head, but I hadn't even gotten as far as my pretend-it's-a-real-kitchen kitchen when the phone rang in my hand. I didn't recognize the number; all the screen told me was it was Boston, Massachusetts, calling. "Sydney Riley."

"Sydney? Oh, hi. It's Karen Hakim."

Ali's sister. Oh, God. My stomach went into freefall. This had to be bad news; that's the only reason Karen would have to call me; she and I had gotten closer over the past summer, but we weren't yet exactly BFFs. So this had to be bad. Ali was dead. He was missing. He'd been shot in the spine and was paralyzed. I'd never see him again. This had to be... "Hi, Karen," I croaked.

"Listen, I only have a moment." Karen is Boston's police commissioner, so I could imagine that was true. Tell me, I pleaded silently. Is it Ali? Is he dead? Why else would his sister call me? His sister never calls me. I'd last seen her when she came to visit in the summer, for Carnival, and we all know how well *that* turned out, Ali shot and in the hospital and nearly bleeding out. . . . And now he was dead. Of course he was dead. *Breathe, Riley, breathe. Just breathe.*

She didn't seem to realize I was in shock. "I was wondering if you have any way to reach Ali," she said.

I struggled to climb out of the grave I'd dug for him in my mind over the past ten seconds. "You mean he's alive?"

"Why wouldn't he be alive?" she asked, startled. "Do you know—"

"No, no. Nothing. It's nothing. I just thought that's why you were calling," I said. Belatedly I realized that sounded churlish, but I'd gone too far down the road to turn back. My heart still felt like it was trying to tear its way out of my chest. "I'm sorry. I just thought you were going to tell me something terrible."

"Oh." She paused, and tried to laugh, but she didn't try hard enough. "Well, it's not terrible, but I do need to reach him. I don't know how."

You're the frigging *police commissioner* of a major metropolitan area and you don't know how to communicate with someone in ICE? This didn't sound much like interagency cooperation to me. "He left me a number," I said. "It's only voicemail, and it's not his, I think, but someone monitors it once a day and can handle emergencies."

"I have that number," she said, her voice impatient. "It's ICE. I thought he had a mobile of his own."

Did he? "That's the only number I have," I said slowly.

There was a pause, and then she said, almost diffidently, "It's our father."

"What's happened?" If she was going to scare me out of my wits, I thought, she could at least tell me why.

"Um, he—well, it's probably nothing, really. I think—his heart is weak, he had an attack a few years back, and I stupidly told him Ali's undercover."

"It wasn't stupid," I said, feeling awkward. I wasn't used to being the one reassuring Karen. She's intimidating as hell. Beautiful, smart, and then there's always that commissioner-of-police thing. "He had to know why Ali wasn't calling." Ali called his parents once a week, no matter what. So did Karen; they were both respectful, dutiful. I should probably tell my mother about that, come to think of it; it might make her like Ali more. "What did Ali tell him? Before he went—" I couldn't think of the word. Under? Into?

"He just said it was an assignment, and he'd be out of touch. But it's been a while, and I think they're starting to imagine things. I was hoping I could get a message through from him."

They hadn't known the worst. Hadn't known that Ali had been shot. Hadn't know he'd come close to dying. He and Karen had both been adamant about that. She'd told them he was on vacation during the time he was in the hospital. I cleared my throat. "Join the club," I said. "I'd love to get a message from him, myself."

"You haven't heard anything?"

I shook my head, a ridiculous thing to do when on the phone. "I'm scared, too," I said.

"I know." There was a pause, as though she were debating whether to go on. "We almost lost him, Sydney," she said, her voice tight. "I don't want to feel like that again."

We almost lost him… Wait: Karen Hakim, vulnerable? It was a whole new slant on her. And… "we"?

She said something indistinct to someone presumably in the same room and then was back. "All right. Do me a favor, Sydney, if you hear from him, please ask him to call me. It's not an emergency. It's just… important." And she disconnected. I stood staring blankly into space. Why hadn't Ali given his sister emergency number in case something like this happened, something with his parents? He knew his father wasn't well, and he already had my vote for the World's Most Dutiful Son. It could only mean his undercover was even more dangerous than I'd assumed, and I'd assumed pretty dire things. *Breathe, Riley, just breathe.* At least things had to improve. My day couldn't possibly get any worse than this.

Of course it could.

<h1 style="text-align:center">15</h1>

While I was on a roll with the phone, I called Helen and arranged to pick her up and drive her down to the pier when they brought the Bessie G in. They weren't actually going to haul her all the way out, at least not onto land or anything like that, as I'd imagined: there was a special crane with something not entirely unlike a hammock that would support her; how far it was going to be above the waterline was anybody's guess.

The police, Craig had said, wanted to be the first to take a look at what was probably going to be considered a crime scene. I noticed everyone seemed to believe the same thing, that Sarah and the girls were going to be on board. It didn't explain Tony, but it explained the other half of the mystery. As to which branch of the police, that was still an unknown; apparently there was some issue about jurisdiction, with Provincetown police, the state police, and the Coast Guard all weighing in.

Lawyers were going to get involved. There was no way lawyers weren't going to get involved.

And Guy Husband. He was already involved. I was feeling unsettled about him. I'd liked him when we first met, when he was talking about the Mignonette, about his passion. But he'd gone from underwater adventurer to friend-of-the-town helper seemingly overnight. What was he getting out of raising the Bessie G? In the grand scheme of things, this was small potatoes compared with his mission of discovering a second pirate ship. Why had he diverted his energy—and a far from trivial amount of money—to bring a mere fishing boat up? He could have been spending his time getting soundings off the Mignonette instead of the Bessie G. Wasn't that why he'd come to P'town?

Something was going on there.

In the meantime, I had a few hours to myself, and I wrapped myself up as warmly as I could and headed down to Commercial Street. It was Holly Folly, and I wasn't about to miss it.

***

They raised the Bessie G.

I got home with packages, way too many of them—Holly Folly is the last hurrah for a lot of the local retailers and artisans before they close up shop until April, a lot of them in their retail spaces and still others at stalls at the Canteen's Winter Holiday Market, and it's important to me to patronize them as much as I can afford to. I had a quick coffee and snuggle with Ibsen before heading out again to pick up the Little Green Car and Helen Correia, in that order.

Helen was waiting for me just inside her door, already dressed for the outdoors and clearly distressed, picking at invisible lint on her coat, taking her gloves off and putting them on again, tucking stray bits of hair under her woolen hat. It had a pompom, that hat, and looked ridiculously festive, not quite striking the right note for the occasion, like a Christmas elf at a funeral. Helen was pretty elfin herself, actually, now that I thought of it, slight with those wisps of dark hair and the luminous Botticelli eyes. She looked thoroughly frightened, and I felt a rush of sympathy. I don't have a brother, so I don't know what it's like to lose one; but Helen's loss was palpable in the still-cold air between us. I spared Karen Hakim a sympathetic thought as I looked into Helen's eyes.

The Little Green Car's heater takes a while to fully get going. "Are you sure you want to go, Helen?" I asked. "You don't have to, you know. They'll tell you what's there anyway, Roger or Julie or somebody's sure to tell you. You don't have to look for yourself if it's too painful."

She stared at me. "Wouldn't *you* want to know?"

I sighed. "Yeah, I guess I would, you put it like that."

Helen nodded. "I have to see it," she said. "I have to know… because I've always imagined the worst, don't you know. All these years, I've imagined so many things that coulda happened. I've thought about it going down, everybody thinks that sometimes, especially when they're late in or the weather turns." She was looking out the window, not at me. "The Race out there," she said. "I been thinking all this time it was the Race. Everyone's afraid of it in bad weather. But that wasn't where they found it."

I was missing something. "The Race?"

A quick glance. "You work down to the Race Point Inn," she said. "How d'you think Race Point got its name?"

I hadn't given it any thought whatsoever. How does anything get its name? "I don't know."

"The Race, that's the current out there, where the bay meets the ocean. It's a real word. Tidal race, something like that. It's why there were so many wrecks, before they built the canal. Was a time, every vessel traveling along the coast between Boston and everywhere to the south had to get through the Race. Now only the fishermen still do." The ferries and the whale watch boats apparently didn't figure in.

I contemplated this for a moment. "But there aren't many that get lost at sea now, right?" I said. "I mean, the boats go through the Race all the time." Can't say I don't adapt quickly to new vocabulary. "And besides, with all the technology you have—even what they had eight years ago." I paused. "Even if they were on board, Helen, even if the boat was sinking, surely they'd have called for help? Put on life jackets, waited for the Coast Guard?"

Helen was back to picking at her hair. She had a section of it and ran it through her mouth. "No life jackets," she said. "And I don't think Sarah could swim. The girls, maybe. But—"

"Why no life jackets?"

She let go of the strand of hair and looked at me. "Don't know about the jackets; Tony never held with them. Anyway, lots of fishermen can't swim," she said. "You go into the Atlantic, you're dead already, don't you know. Best not to fight it, let it happen. That's what most people think."

I couldn't contradict her. I've been in the harbor in October—not voluntarily, but that's another story for another day—and immediately understood everything I ever needed to know about hypothermia. And that was the *harbor*, not miles offshore in the Atlantic Ocean. They'd freeze before anyone got to them. I wondered which death was worse, freezing or drowning. I wondered which was more merciful.

Helen was pursuing her own thoughts. "She was our father's boat, the Bessie G, don't you know," she said, looking out the window at Bradford Street. "Tony inherited her, like, but had to mortgage her twice for repairs'n such. But she was our father's, an' he used to have a crew. Back when the fleet was something to see. Now there's only twelve Eastern rigs on the east coast, but back then, there were a lot more of 'em. The harbor was full. When they was all in port at the same time… well, it was a sight. It was a sight for sure." She sighed. "I'm remembering—we're talking the seventies, now—there was more than seventy boats workin' out of Provincetown. They tied up at the pier, four'n five boats deep sometimes. If you ever meet anybody who worked on the Bessie G back in my father's time, they'll have stories to tell… They all loved working that boat. Different times, don't you know."

I'd imagined it before. My elderly Portuguese neighbor had told me the stories often enough. Of fish stretching out silvery and glittering and so very plentiful you could almost believe you could walk across the bay. The cousins from the Azores coming in to fish for the season, when a place on a boat meant financial security for a year. The light on the water, that aching light on the water, the seamless ballet of men moving around the deck, the grace of the nautical gear they used, muscles and boredom and fear and hard work.

Different times.

The pier was, to my surprise, not terribly crowded, and nearly all the people were locals, most of them from or related in some way to the fishing community; this was one of their own. I'm not sure a lot of washashores would feel welcome; I was pretty sure no visitors would.

No one was taking, chatting idly while they waited, the way you'd expect; but the silence was charged with energy. It was the kind of silence you feel when you walk into a cathedral, vibrating with centuries of intense, focused prayer, retaining the myriad breaths that had breathed in its incense, throwing back across the years the magic of ritual until you felt you were part of an ancient and mysterious story. There was that focus here, that intensity.

Provincetown is the second-largest natural deep-water harbor in the world (or so my friend Pat Medina, who drives the Mayflower Trolley and narrates the Provincetown tour, informs me), and it needed to be, for Guy's exploration vessel—fetchingly called Gargantua, in either a nod to Rabelais or some bizarre competition with Robert Whittier's Giant Explorer—was probably using up every inch of it. Or fathom. Or however they measure water. (Surely not by the gallon?)

I live at the seaside and I don't know how to measure water. There's probably something profoundly wrong about that.

The wind was truly biting out here; the only time I'd felt it worse was been when there'd been a blizzard, when it added particles of ice to scratch your face into the mix. This day had turned clear, with all its edges sharp and merciless and a sun that did nothing to warm—and that wind just kept coming straight off the water.

No one but me seemed to be noticing. They all stood still, huddled and silent, watching the shipping lane left of Long Point Light, waiting for the Gargantua to come around it, following the route taken by the fast ferries that ply the water between Boston and Provincetown all summer, the shipping lane that eventually brought all P'town's sailors back to port.

Or didn't. There aren't many widow's walks in Provincetown; our connection to the sea is a blue-collar one. Up in Newburyport, in Portsmouth, the clipper ships' captains built sumptuous mansions in which their wives could wait and worry; those women were wearing silks and jewels as they paced widow's walks looking out to sea, and had servants who brought them something warmer to slip around their shoulders. Here the women who waited? They worked, too, loading fish, cutting fish, freezing fish. They scrubbed municipal buildings, ran shops, nursed the sick, taught school, took in sewing, raised children. But no matter what else they did, they waited. They watched the tides and the skies and when the lights they were waiting for rounded Long Point, their faces lit up, too, and they breathed more deeply.

It was years of that waiting, generations of that waiting, that I was feeling that afternoon on MacMillan wharf. It was the culmination of women watching the weather, watching the water, listening for rumors, reaching for their rosary beads. A long-awaited boat was finally coming home to port.

With, perhaps, *an* answer—if not *the* answer—people were waiting for.

***

Helen was completely stoic.

I hadn't expected anything else, not really: that's another thing about the women. Commercial fishing is the second-most dangerous occupation in the world, and when you live under the shadow of that knowledge you have to find a way to cope or you'll go crazy. Most of them are calm; most of them endure.

She'd stopped playing with her hat and her hair, plucking at her coat; her hands had stilled, and if anything I could swear that her breathing had slowed. This was the last bit, the last mile, the last moment before everything would—or wouldn't—change for her, and she was completely conscious of it. She was strong. She was dignified. She was amazing.

We parked in the small strip of places beside the harbormaster's office and stepped outside into the cold, and I couldn't detect a change of expression on her face: she looked as frozen as the ice on the railings. Above us, gulls wheeled and screamed.

The hush didn't last; all of a sudden, it seemed, the sound of the engines engulfed us, bouncing off the breakwater, magnified in the still frigid air. I shivered and pushed my hands farther down into my pockets. Most people were watching the lane, but slowly they started noticing Helen, an elbow jabbed into someone's midriff, a whisper quickly silenced. For this one moment, perhaps, everyone gets to be royalty.

When they saw Helen, they moved away, the crowd parting naturally and silently, letting us go through, to the end of the pier, to where the Gargantua was heading; a couple of people touched her arm or murmured something to her. She gave no indication of hearing or feeling anything; she had that same trancelike focus now, too. There was nothing but her and the Bessie G.

And just a few ghosts.

As the ship approached—and damn, was it big—I was mildly surprised to see the size of the *crew*; I had no idea how Guy got so many people to work for him under these cold conditions. Paid them well, more than likely; I wondered how they felt about this diversion from their main mission. The Bessie G was dwarfed by the ship. She hung off the back of it crossways, supported by all sorts of canvas and metal contraptions, looking the worse for wear for sure, but better than I'd expected—though I really don't know what exactly I'd imagined. Covered in shells and barnacles and mysterious marine growth than I couldn't identify; even the shape wasn't quite right.

She still had the long and lean lines of an Eastern rig, with the wheelhouse in the back rather than the front, unlike most of the other fishing boats I saw every day at MacMillan. Her paint—a sort of aqua and white scheme—was still vaguely visible, and even her rigging and trawl winch seemed to be intact.

But she looked so tiny, like a discarded child's toy, like something too small to have ever attempted to go out to George's or Stellwagen or whatever underwater mountain range it was she went to find fish. Beside the ship, she could have been a lifeboat, creaky and superannuated and beyond its useful lifetime, being retired after long service.

Without looking at her, without thinking, I put an arm around Helen's shoulders. I wasn't sure what would be the right thing to do, but she didn't twitch it off, so I left it there. Beneath my arm, she was still as a statue.

They didn't turn off the Gargantua's engines, even once she was in place and her lines made fast, powering who knew what else on the vessel, and it was loud as hell, the sound ricocheting off the pier and the breakwater and the few fishing boats in their berths; everything seemed to spit the sound right back at us. Like some of the cruise ships that anchor or tie up here in the summer, it dwarfed the pier and the people on it, towering and almost majestic, though with a hint of something very modern and more than a little scary.

Helen's jawline was hard. She had finally moved, slightly; I could feel her bracing herself.

A stream of official-looking people came out of the harbormaster's office and filed across the pier and boarded the ship; there was a Coast Guard cutter idling nearby, and it headed in and people boarded from the other side. Not entirely unlike Sam Bellamy and his merry men, I found myself thinking involuntarily, the pirate museum at my back; boarding parties and the very real question of whose authority would win out.

I didn't care, frankly. What I cared about now, and found I cared rather fiercely, was that they did right by Helen. Helen, and all the other people gathered here, shivering in the sun, noses reddened by the wind, waiting silently to find out what had happened to some of their own.

I touched Helen's arm. "Did Sarah have family?" I whispered; it was that kind of atmosphere, where to speak loudly would have been to shatter a spell, like shouting in church. I was thinking that if Sarah's family were here, then the news they were waiting for was probably even more urgent than what it seemed to Helen;

she had, after all, been able to bury her brother. I found myself holding my breath, surreptitiously looking more closely at some of the faces in the crowd that I didn't know, wondering if any of them could be her kin, wondering why I hadn't thought to ask Helen that already.

She shook her head. She wasn't looking at me; she hadn't taken her eyes off the Bessie G. "Killed in a road accident up to the bridge, don't you know," she said. "Ten or twelve years before all this happened." She paused. "I'm all that's left."

I nodded and let my breath out into the air in a cloud of white mist, tightening my arm around her shoulder for a moment. That was something, anyway; no one here was about to find out a sister or daughter had been killed. The pain would be communal, not personal.

Except, of course, for Helen herself.

It seemed a long time, but in fact was probably no more than half an hour after they tied up before someone came down the gangway from the Gargantua; it was Guy Husband himself. He was searching the faces on the pier, and lighted on us almost at once. "Ms. Correia," he said, and held out his hand. "I'm Guy Husband, I'm in charge of this operation. Would you be so kind as to accompany me on board?"

This *operation?*

Helen turned to me, finally disengaging her gaze from the boat, now hanging significantly above us; I could feel her anxiety coming at me in waves. I kept my arm around her shoulder. Guy was watching her, and cleared his throat. "And Ms. Riley, too, of course," he said smoothly, and she nodded and took my hand and pulled me along behind her.

The gangway felt none too stable beneath us—just that little bit of aluminum between me and the harbor, and I'd had far too many involuntary dunkings in said harbor to not take it seriously—and then we were on board. A knot of men was waiting for us there: Roger, the harbormaster, and a couple of guys in Coast Guard uniforms, and a couple of other guys who were in civilian clothes but whose haircuts and manner screamed police. Julie Agassi wasn't among them; obviously, Provincetown police were off the case. I resented that on her behalf. This was our town; these were our people. She should have been there.

It might have looked cruise-like from the dock, but once you were on board, there was no mistaking the Gargantua for anything but a serious working environment. There was equipment—huge equipment, I can't even find words for the scale of this—on deck whose uses I couldn't even guess at, winches and coils of steel hawser and cranes and all of it dirty enough to be in working order. Guy's "operation."

Helen wasn't seeing any of it. Her eyes were on the stern. On the Bessie G.

Guy stayed with us, and kept talking. "As you see, we were able to raise her gently," he said, a nicety for which I immediately gave him several points. I know they assign boats the female gender, but this sounded like something more than that, something deeper. It was as though he were talking about a person rather than a thing. To the Correias, to the fishing community, that could well have been true: the boat wasn't just a means of livelihood, it was an extension of the family. It was what made them who they'd been. There's a reason, I thought suddenly, that boats are mostly given human names.

I still didn't see what it had to do with finding pirate treasure.

Helen had eyes only for the fishing boat. And in fact now that I was closer, it was extraordinary how really good the Bessie G looked. As though it would only take a thorough cleaning and then she could be lowered into the water and motor off again, ready for a day's work offshore.

There were a number of people on board close to us, and even on the wide deck it was feeling a little cramped. Two of them were wearing the white suits you see the forensics teams wearing on television, moving about in a way that indicated competence, eyes down, intent, carrying mysterious tools, going up and down the very steep gangway between the Gargantua's deck and that of the Bessie G. Someone had brought some strong arc lights to bear on the superstructure and they illuminated it, even in this bright daylight, with a kind of sinister cast, something way too bright and sharp, a movie set gone terribly wrong. Suddenly the whole thing, the whole "expedition," seemed wrong to me, pulling the boat up out of the sea, subjecting it to this examination, like an elderly patient being poked and prodded in an emergency room.

She should have been allowed a little more dignity.

Helen seemed to be holding her breath, and I patted her arm in some sort of inadequate gesture of reassurance. Guy cleared his throat, again, unnecessarily. "I wonder if you'd like to speak with the investigator," he said, almost diffidently. "He's not ready for any kind of formal report, of course, but would be happy to tell you whatever it is he feels he can share at this time—"

"I want to see it," Helen said. "I want to go on board." She was still looking at the boat, her eyes scanning it, back and forth, as though something would move, something would catch her gaze, she was so intent that I looked up, too, half-expecting to see Tony Correia heading back to the wheelhouse, feeling the presence of Sarah and the girls on deck, helping the nets, wearing gumboots and slickers and laughing at something one of them had just said.

I pulled my gaze away and glanced at Guy; he was looking unhappy. "Oh, dear. Ms.

Correia, that's just not on. I'm afraid that insurance regulations forbid—"

She rounded on him then, jerkily, a marionette whose strings had been pulled abruptly, forcefully, and it broke the spell; when I glanced back up at the Bessie G there were no more fanciful images of dead people there. "You think I'm going to break my neck falling into the boat?" Helen was demanding. "You worried that someone's gonna *sue* you? I've been on an' off that boat, mister, for most of my life. I know it like I know my own house, maybe even better. An' don't start on me contaminating no scene, neither. It's been under water. There isn't nothin' I can do to mess it up any more now."

She had a good point, though you also had to give television some credit for her vocabulary. Not sure that twenty years ago anyone would have thought about contaminating a scene. Guy was hesitating. I said, quickly, "It can't hurt for her to just take a look, Guy," as though it were the most reasonable request in the world. He was looking at me as though I'd started foaming at the mouth.

In the end, though, he must have known what would happen, must have known it well before he'd brought us on board the Gargantua or he wouldn't have bothered. I wondered if this were all a game for her benefit, play-acting to make her think she'd scored a point, though I didn't know why that would be the case. But there was no way he was going to stand up to a middle-aged spinster from a Portuguese fishing family; she would have worn him down no matter what his original intentions were. I didn't think that in his myriad and no doubt significant business dealings worldwide he'd had a lot of experience with people like Helen Correia.

Welcome to Provincetown.

They'd established an incredibly shaky-looking aluminum bridge across and up to the Bessie G, steep as hell, bridging the space between the deck of the exploration vessel and the fishing boat dangling above it, hanging off the aft supported by a tremendous two-sided crane-like machine. I have no idea what these things are called. It was solid, which was good, as it rather looked like the boat could disintegrate at any moment.

A guy in dark blue Coast Guard fatigues gave Helen a hand onto the gangway, which she barely needed; she'd been right, she'd clearly grown up in this environment. She made it look like a walk in the park, her pace regular and brisk. She looked like she was climbing a skyscraper that was off to the side from another skyscraper. I considered leaving her to it. My feet felt leaden.

"You can go," Guy said quietly, standing beside me.

Oh, thanks, I was just waiting for your permission. I didn't say that; what I said was, "I'm not sure I should." Okay, aside from the whole not wanting to climb up a glorified metal ladder thing, and we won't even mention ghosts, which I was pretty sure the boat was full of, I was actually conflicted in some other ways. Part of me wanted to be with Helen; she'd chosen me as her accomplice, representative, whatever, and that was why I was present. I was supposed to be beside her, ready to help with whatever was waiting. And there was another part of me that went back a few weeks, remembering stumbling sad and lonely across the parking lot, the blaze of the sodium vapor lighting and the infinite sadness of how Pete had ended up there. Unaccountably, I wanted to cry.

Then Helen stood up straighter on the deck and looked over at me, doing everything but tapping a toe to show she was waiting, and that pretty much made the decision for me. They weren't my ghosts to face, they were hers, and I was being a total self-centered bitch about this whole thing. All I had to do was climb up the gangway. That's all.

Ready or not…

I took a deep breath and headed up the very fragile-feeling temporary structure, which swayed alarmingly under me and was at much more of an angle even than it had looked from below. One foot after the next, that was all it would take. I hoped. Okay, I'm not going to scream. Such a girlie thing to do, screaming. *Just breathe, Riley*, I told myself. *Just breathe and you'll be all right.*

I don't know about being all right, but at least it got me up that damned thing and across to the Bessie G.

An Eastern rig is totally out of style these days—chances are if you ever visit any fishing port, you won't see any of them, fishing fleets these days all have the wheelhouse forward, toward the front of the boat. The Eastern rig started out when fishing boats were transitioning from sail to engine and from hooks to nets, and for the time was quite the thing, the essence of modernity. I was frantically reciting these facts to myself as I inched across the Bessie G's deck, more than—I'll admit it—a little afraid. But I'd looked it up online, and it was easier to recite facts than to think about standing on the deck of a ghost ship. The Bessie G, I knew from my research, could easily fish with a crew of three, and do it fast. She dragged a big fishnet, oddly called an otter trawl, along the seabed and pulled up treasure: cod, haddock, flounder, whatever was on offer.

There are no ghosts on board. There are absolutely no ghosts on board.

Some days I wish I were still a practicing Catholic. There's something comforting about having an arsenal of material ready at your fingertips to help you navigate any occasion. It would make far more sense, for example, to say a Hail Mary or two—rather than reciting Wikipedia entries back at myself when in distress or crisis. A real Catholic could summon help—a saint, perhaps, or a guardian angel. Something like that.

Helen was looking at me oddly, and I wondered if perhaps I'd been turning a little green. I was still reverberating from walking up that gangway—how much sway is normal in those things?—but the thought of what, or more precisely whom, might still be on the Bessie G along with us was fluttering around inside my stomach. I don't really believe in ghosts. Not really. The guy in blue fatigues was standing off to the side, watching us, and I felt rather than heard Guy Husband move up behind me. "I'm here," I said to her, unnecessarily and a little too heartily. Maybe everyone would think I was turning green on Helen's behalf.

She nodded, her lips compressed, and turned to the hatch. She was a lot stronger than me; I wondered, fleetingly, why she wanted me there. "I'm going down below," she informed the seaman.

He's obviously expected it and was ready with both a hand and a giant flashlight. "Watch your step, ma'am," he said, guiding her to the top of the stairway. Me, he left to fend for myself. I must look a lot more able-bodied than I sometimes feel.

It was remarkably strange, standing on that deck, old and worn, just feet away from the shining modern expanse of the Gargantua. I could almost feel the presence of the others, the men who had piloted it through rough seas, the guys pulling up the nets with the catch exploding onto the deck, back in the days when the sea was still rich and catches were still plentiful. They'd built this boat and they'd made a living off her, one of the most difficult and dangerous livings in the world, and they'd always somehow come back to port.

And now, five years late, the Bessie G had done it one last time. Tony hadn't brought her home, as he had for years; but she was home again for all of that. There was something catching at my throat at the thought.

I grasped the bulkhead and pulled myself into the wheelhouse, the stairs—if you could call them that— disappearing below me into a darkness spiked with a flashlight's beam. They hadn't rigged those bright lights down here, yet.

Helen was already on the ladder they'd rigged to go down into the hold, having demonstrated a surprising nimbleness; she was older than me, but I can't move that fast. Besides, she knew this boat, probably had moved about it in pitch-blackness since she was three years old. I wasn't quite as nimble, and my fingers were scrabbling for a railing or anything to cling to, and of course I caught my toe and descended a lot faster than I'd intended.

From beside me, another powerful flashlight came alive and picked out my face, which was enormously helpful, the light bright and blinding. "Watch your step," said the man behind it, perhaps one of Guy's guys. Watch my step? What did he *think* I was doing? That I'd tripped just for the hell of it? That I *hadn't* been watching my step?

He swung the light around and beyond the shadow that was Helen I saw the inside curving sides of the boat—people slept down here? It was cramped as hell, and everything coated with a lichen-like seaweed that seemed to be undulating. I looked more closely and saw a crab moving. There was something that could have been a counter, or a shelf, back in better days, and… and then the flashlight moved lower down, down to the floor, itself covered with debris and algae. But there was no mistaking what was in the center of it all.

A skull.

16

And so Sarah Correia, who would have turned forty-three this year, and Charlotte Correia, who would have made it to eighteen, and Maria Correia, who would just have passed her fourteenth birthday, came home to Provincetown.

I had to pry Helen out of the Bessie G. I had a feeling she was really close to losing it.

"They're going to bring them out," I told her. "They're going to take good care of them. They're going to treat them with respect." Okay, so I was making assumptions here, but they were probably true. They had to be true.

Helen had sunk to her knees and now, tentatively, reached out to touch the skull. It was achingly small; one of the girls. That got a reaction from the guy with the flashlight. "Don't touch anything!"

"It's my family," Helen said in a tight voice that had a sharp, dangerous edge to it.

"It's a crime scene," he said.

She gasped, and I put my arm around her shoulders and started trying to get her to stand up. "Come on, Helen. You've seen it, you've seen what you came to see. There isn't anything you can do right now. Let them do their work."

"I can't leave them alone!" She half-turned to look at me, her hands clutching my coat sleeves. "Sydney. Don't you see? They've been alone all this time. All these years. All alone. Tony wasn't with them, I wasn't with them, no one was down here with them. I can't leave them alone now."

"They won't be alone," I said. I closed my hand over hers. "Listen to me. Look at me, Helen, look at me." Her eyes were blurred, unfocused. "There are people here who'll take good care of them, Helen, I promise. And you'll be able to see them again. Once they're out, you'll be able to see them again." I had no idea whether or not that was true, but it was all I had to offer.

"Are they... are all... is everyone here?"

The man behind the flashlight said, not ungently, "There are the remains of three individuals, ma'am."

"Oh, God," said Helen. She sagged against me. I wondered if she'd held out hope, all these years, that they might somehow be coming home, alive and well and filled with sparkling stories of a foreign trip, a shipwrecked island, an adventure that kept them young and happy and alive. I wondered if she'd been able to bear her grief over her brother by telling herself that the family lived on, the fishing boat lived on, the name was not forgotten. I wondered how much it was costing her to know the truth.

But even as I pulled Helen against me and moved her toward the stairs, all I could think was, so what? How much farther along were we now? What did this tell us? That the Bessie G had gone down. That Sarah and the children had died in it. But how that connected to Tony and the bullet in *his* skull was still as mysterious as ever.

The guy with the flashlight was herding us to the stairs, such as they were, and I propelled Helen ahead of me. The hold suddenly seemed smaller, claustrophobic, its secrets tight and dark. Death had happened here, violent death had happened here, and we were the first people to hear its echoes, to smell its scent, to feel its breath. I sensed it looking over our shoulders, following us out, and my spine felt frozen. Even the knife-sharp cold air outside felt welcome.

I focused on following Helen, on putting one foot in front of the other, never raising my eyes from the gangway, that irrational fear still at my back, resisting an urge to push her forward fast and start running. I'd have put us both in the harbor if I had, but the fear was there, still.

There was a murmur from the group clustered on the pier as soon as Helen appeared. Nothing overt, just a sense of sharpened attention, of focus, of anticipation. Guy walked her formally across the deck of the Gargantua, one hand lightly below her elbow. I was again assumed to be capable of independent perambulation. I wasn't sure if I ought to feel complimented or insulted.

And, man, was it cold.

The group parted as Helen stepped onto the wharf and then moved back into place, smoothly, absorbing her effortlessly into their mass, drawing the line firmly: she was one of them. No one said anything to her; it was almost eerie. Someone's arm went up around her shoulders and she virtually disappeared.

I stayed at the top of the gangway, shivering and watching; she clearly didn't need me now, and I was a little at a loss as to what to do next. Guy stood beside me. "A bit anticlimactic, wouldn't you say?" he asked.

I glanced over at him, but couldn't see his face; he was busily lighting a cigarette. "Not for the people back there," I said.

He straightened and blew out smoke. "It doesn't mean their story will be told," he said. "We may never know their story."

"So why did you do it?"

He didn't look at me. "What do you mean?"

"You know what I mean," I said. I turned and faced him. "You're supposed to be here to research a pirate ship," I said. "This doesn't look like a pirate ship."

"Did Mirela put you up to this?"

I was startled. "Of course not. The last I saw of Mirela…" And then it hit me. The last I'd seen of Mirela, she was madly painting images of three bodies that were trapped and screaming. Before anyone had seen what was on the Bessie G. Some sixth sense had kept her tuned in to what was happening. This was more than a little creepy.

Guy was waiting for an answer. "The last I saw of Mirela," I said firmly, "she was working all night in her studio. She seemed disturbed. To say the least. But I suppose you'd know more about that than I do." I winced even as the words came out; I sounded completely jealous of Guy. That was unexpected. I tried a different tack. "Why would Mirela put me up to anything, anyway?"

"She thinks I shouldn't have raised the boat."

"You still haven't said why you did," I reminded him. "This had to have been staggeringly expensive, this whole thing, so you must have had a really good reason."

"Yes," he said, and his voice was as distant as the horizon. "Yes, I must have done, must'n I." But it wasn't a question. He was watching Helen, and then his eyes turned back to me with a snap that could almost be felt. "I won't keep you any longer, Sydney," he said.

I knew when I was being dismissed. I grasped the gangway and prayed I wasn't going to slip on it. I was either going to have to get better around boats or move away from the seaside.

Not that the Gargantua was a boat; even I could perceive that. I was about two stories over the pier, and while apart from a couple of Underground stations in London I've never particularly had a fear of heights, I was clearly making an exception now. As I looked down I could see myself falling, exactly as though it had already happened, and it was as though I were being drawn down, and damn it, I've spent far too much time in that harbor in the off-season already. *Breathe, Riley.*

And then a hand closed over mine on the railing and Craig was standing there, cheerful and reassuring. "Hey, Sydney. Why don't I just slip on here ahead of you, and we can go down together?"

An angel from heaven couldn't have been more welcome. I tried blasé, aware that I was totally not pulling it off, and not even caring "Hey, Craig. Sure, that would be fine."

He shouldered past me and held out a hand. "Come on."

I took it, clinging to the aluminum railing with my other hand, and feeling the sway of the gangway under us. Why had it seemed so much easier going up? But Craig kept talking, inching how way down, holding tightly to my hand, an ongoing patter about the size of the ship and how it was the second-biggest ever tied at MacMillan since he'd been with the harbormaster's office, and what a crisp day it was but we should watch out because there was snow in the forecast but Holly Folly would be over before that happened and…. I stopped listening halfway down, just letting the tide of words wash over me, the calmness of them, the ordinariness, feeling like I just might make it after all.

"You are my hero," I said, gratefully, once my feet were on *terra firma*—or as *firma* a *terra* as a pier ever gets.

"No worries," he said cheerfully. "Just don't ever apply for a job with us."

"Last thing on my mind," I agreed with some fervor.

Helen was waiting for me, impatient now that she was back on the pier, aware of all the curious onlookers. "Can we go?"

It felt almost like the famous perp walk from all the crime shows on TV, even down to a reporter with microphone in hand and cameraman trailing behind. The Boston stations hadn't wasted any time. "Ms. Correia, what did you see? Was your family on board the Bessie G?"

"Leave her alone," I said, my arm linked through Helen's, and giving him an elbow in the microphone for good measure. *Record that*, I thought uncharitably. I didn't like the easy familiarity with which he'd said, Bessie G, as if he'd known about her all along, as if the name belonged to him.

Maybe it did, now.

We made it to the Little Green Car and I started the engine and coaxed the heater into doing its thing. "Do you want to go home?" I asked.

She seemed a million miles away. "The ice maker was still there," she said.

"Okay," I said cautiously. I wouldn't know a commercial ice maker from a microwave. And anyway, everything seemed encrusted with something—Guy would know the term for it— that nothing looked like anything but lumps. Still, Helen would know. "Is that significant?"

She glanced at me, finally realizing where she was. "What? No, of course not." She drew her coat even more tightly around herself. "Take me home."

17

I was still restless, and there was that faint worry about Mirela in the back of my mind, so as soon as Helen was safely ensconced among her memories, I headed over to the studio. I didn't call ahead; I didn't want to give her any excuse to put me off.

Just as well. When she opened the door it was clear she'd been crying; and all the horrible death scenes were stacked in a corner. "What happened? Mirela, what is it?"

"I do not even know," she said. Her voice sounded empty; there was an echo in it, as if she hadn't used it much lately. It was sad beyond words. "I think perhaps it is time I go home for a while."

"I have the Little Green Car," I told her. "I can give you a lift, we can talk."

She smiled, a wintry smile that underlined what my stomach was already telling me. "I do not mean here," she said. "I mean Plovdiv."

Things were going from bad to worse, if Mirela was thinking of going back to Bulgaria. She never talked about Plovdiv. (I actually thought at first she was making that name up.) What she usually said, when I suggested it, was that she'd been a different person then. I personally thought it would be a delightful trip I could take with her sometime in the spring or fall, and she always laughed at me. "I will return to Plovdiv when I die," was all she'd say.

It didn't bode well for her state of mind, anyway. "You are exhausted," I said fiercely. "This isn't a time to be making plans." I gestured to the paintings stacked in the corner. "I don't know what was going on there, Mirela, but you can't base anything on that."

She shrugged and turned away. "You want tea, sunshine?"

I closed the door behind me. "Sure," I said, a little helplessly. I had no idea what was going on. "Do you know what you were painting?"

She had the kettle on the countertop stove. "What do you mean?"

I nodded my head toward the stack. Mirela never stacks her canvases. "That."

"It was a bad dream," she said slowly. "I could not get it from my head."

"What? What did you dream?" She looked at me a little vaguely and I wanted to shake her. "Mirela, Guy brought up the Bessie G, and there were bodies inside."

"Guy," she said, and nodded.

This time I did it; I walked across the studio and took her arm and gave it a shake. "Mirela. Snap out of it," I said. "You're scaring me."

Her eyes found my face and she focused. "Yes," she said, and shed the wooliness from her voice. "It is because of Guy," she said.

"What happened?" I guided her over to one of her few decent chairs and pulled over a more rickety one for myself. "Tell me what's going on," I said. I'd meant to sound gentle, but the words were a command, not a request.

It worked, anyway. She seemed to gather herself. "He has not found the Mignonette," she said. "He is very frustrated. I think he thought it would be easy, and it is not. And he is not alone, now."

"What do you mean?" I had visions of a wife suddenly appearing out of the woodwork.

"It is a rumor, perhaps only a rumor, I do not know, but they are saying that Robert Whittier is returning. In March." She took a breath. "To explore the Mignonette, just as he explored the Whydah."

Well, that answered one question, anyway: why Guy Husband was looking for a wreck in December. I remembered his voice when he was driving me to Orleans, the competition between them, the schadenfreude as he recounted Whittier's problems. He wasn't about to let the other man beat him to the wreck he thought of as his own. "So that's why the Gargantua is here."

She nodded. "But he is more and more upset, because he knows it is here, the Mignonette. Yet he has been unsuccessful. He has—I do not understand it all—side-scan sonar he is putting down, every day, but there is nothing." She looked at me. "What if it is not there, after all?"

"Something is," I said. "There've been artifacts washed up." What were they? I couldn't remember; the Bessie G. had driven everything else from my mind. I needed a conversation with John.

Gold, I remembered. That one gold coin in John's pocket; more, no doubt, in Guy's possession. Gold, echoes of greed and fear and death coming up through the centuries. Then as now, people would kill—and die—for gold.

Mirela shrugged. "Perhaps," she said. "But I will tell you this, sunshine. I think Guy knows more than he is saying."

"About what?"

A helpless gesture. "That is just it! I do not know! He has secrets."

I said, a little uncomfortably, "You know, you and Guy, that's new. Maybe he doesn't feel right sharing everything with you yet." I had no idea what I was talking about.

She looked at me pityingly. "Sunshine," she said, "Do you not think I know that? We are not getting married. We are not staying together. It is a lovely thing, but that is all. This is not about romance. This is about him paying so much attention to a fishing boat, when he should be paying attention to the Mignonette. March is coming quickly. And every day he is out on the water is costing him a lot of money. Why waste any of it? He is not the sort to waste anything, I think."

And there it was again. Why did Guy want to raise the Bessie G? Especially now that I knew about Robert Whittier's possible interest, I'd have thought he'd become even more single-minded about the wreck.

What was on the Bessie G?

*****

There are certain places in Provincetown where you can be sure to catch the gossip. One of them is the post office—at least half the population uses a post office box for mail, due partly to the need to move twice a year from the nice winter apartment to some other digs while one's apartment is rented out by the week in the season; and due partly to the need for companionship. The second is Stop & Shop, where there's at least one conversation for every aisle and a whole lot more at the deli counter. And the third is the soup kitchen.

P'town's soup kitchen is life-saving. If you cannot afford to eat, it's a hot meal in the middle of the day. But it's not limited to those who cannot afford anything else; for a very reasonable cost, anyone can come and eat what is truly delicious food and hang out with friends and neighbors for a while. This time of year, during Holly Folly and into the Christmas season, it's a nice option. Come January and February, it's a necessity.

The next morning I plotted. Ibsen was delighted that I made no move to get out of bed, and curled up close to me, purring. I had a notebook and a pen, and tried to go about things methodically. One column: What we know. Another column: What we think. I scratched Ibsen under the chin and he looked at me adoringly. These moments don't come frequently in our relationship. "It's the royal we," I informed him, and he looked appreciative of being included in the conversation.

My columns didn't develop anything satisfying. I thought about calling my mother and telling her I had a strange disease and couldn't host her for Christmas after all. I thought about trying to reach Ali again. I wondered if Karen had managed to contact him, and whether she'd been able to give their parents any comfort. I wondered what Guy was doing. I considered coloring my hair.

At noon I took a shower, got dressed, and headed over to the Methodist church, where the soup kitchen was already in full swing.

As expected, John was there. I grabbed the empty seat beside him. "Hold this for me, will you?"

He looked bemused. "Sure, Sydney."

I paid the fee and got my trayful of food: tamarind soup, mango and tomato salad, roast pork, jasmine rice, green beans in coconut milk, a piece of coconut cake. I'd probably gain pounds and pounds if I ate here every day.

John was already on his cake. I'd have to talk fast.

"Time to come clean," I told him. "How did you really know Guy Husband?"

He looked startled. "I told you," he said. "I didn't. Guy I knew, knew him."

I swallowed a spoonful of soup and it went down the wrong way and I started coughing. John swatted my back a couple of times. I gulped some water and wiped the tears from my eyes, and by then he's identified his escape route. "See you, Sydney."

"Wait—" But he was already gone.

I took another spoonful of soup, this time more cautiously. Someone sat down in the chair John had just vacated. "Hello, Sydney."

It was Julie Agassi. In uniform. Without a lunch tray. This was business. "Hey, Julie."

"I thought you'd want to know," she said. "They're releasing the information this afternoon. It's about Pete."

I swallowed and pushed the soup away. I was suddenly not very hungry. "And?"

"And he was killed with a boat hook," she said steadily, watching me. I don't think I was actually a viable suspect, it's just the way she looks at anybody when she's wearing her uniform. Waiting to see how they'll respond.

It would be stupid to ask who might have a boat hook in a town that's still at least partly a fishing community. "Who would have a boat hook?" I asked.

Her eyes narrowed and she chose to ignore me. "He wasn't killed where you found him," she said instead. "There would have been a lot of blood."

Neither of us said it. He was on the pier. Where all the commercial boats tied up. All of which got plenty of blood on their decks, and all of which were equipped to hose them off. I swallowed again. "Out at sea?" I asked.

"Possibly." She wasn't giving anything away.

"Did he—was it quick?" I'd liked Pete, just as I liked Craig. They were good guys.

She touched my hand, briefly. "I hope so," she said, and pushed her chair back and stood up. "I just wanted you to know, because I know how much you obsess on these things. There was nothing you could have done. He'd been dead a couple of hours before you found him."

I looked at my plate, unseeing. The really rotten thing was, I *hadn't* been obsessing over Pete. I'd been too caught up in the excitement of pirate treasure and older crimes to spare too many thoughts for someone I'd known, and liked, and found.

Not exactly my finest hour.

"They're going to re-open the Tony Correia case," Julie said, almost as an afterthought. "And enlarge it to include Sarah and the girls." Her voice held familiarity: she'd known them all, personally. The problems of being a cop in a small town.

"Were they shot, too? Like Tony?" I was feeling a little muddled, still castigating myself about Pete.

The official look was in her eyes again. "It's an ongoing investigation," she said gently.

John was waiting for me when I got back to my apartment. "Christ, but it's cold," He said, rubbing his hands together. "You took your time."

"I'm not the one who left lunch like a bat out of hell," I pointed out. "Anyway, why didn't you just go in and wait for me? You've never hesitated before."

"Someone already there."

Okay, I thought this was just a thing in romance novels, but I could swear my heart leapt. Ali! It had to be Ali! I was up the stairs before the thought finished forming in my mind, tearing the door open. He was safe. He was well. He was home.

Helen Correia was sitting at my kitchen table.

I drew in a deep breath. My disappointment must have shown, because she stirred and said, uncomfortably, "I was passing, and thought you might be in."

No one's just passing. Not in the winter-time. I went in and unwound my scarf and took off my coat. "It's fine," I said.

John had followed me up the stairs and shut the door gently behind himself. Helen didn't show any surprise at his presence. "It's father," she said.

"Whose father?" I wasn't in the mood for games. Damn it, I'd really believed there for a moment that it could be Ali.

"Father," she repeated, almost irritated. "At church. At Saint Peter's."

Oh. *That* father. "What about him?"

She wasn't looking at me; she was looking down at her hands, clasped together in her lap. She was dressed all in brown today, which wasn't her color; she looked a little like a sparrow. "He said as you've been helping me, I should—tell you the truth."

I sat down across from her. "You haven't been?" I hadn't picked up on anything. Apparently, as a sleuth, I would do well to keep my job as a wedding planner.

She kept smoothing out her skirt, looking at it as though fascinated. Behind me, I could hear the loveseat springs as John sat down. One day I'd buy a new sofa. "I—no," she said. "I didn't know—I didn't want to betray Tony, don't you know."

"Uh-huh," I said. I had no idea what she was talking about.

"But Father said it was no betrayal. He said justice must be done." She looked up, suddenly, and met my eyes. "And I'd rather tell you than the police, don't you know."

I nodded encouragingly. "So tell me now."

"He found it," she said.

The room went very quiet. I drew in a breath, slowly, silently. "He found what?" I asked, though I already knew. It was the only thing that made sense.

She nodded, as though reading my thoughts. "That wreck," she said. "That pirate ship. He knew where it was."

Behind me, John made some sort of movement on the loveseat; it doesn't allow for silence. I wondered how much of this he already knew. They're both old-school Provincetown, John and Helen. I still didn't know why he was here. "Okay," I said slowly.

She flicked her glance away, back down to her skirt. "Called it his retirement," she said. "Funny, things are. He'd always gone to that spot, scalloping, you know." A glance to see if I were following her. "Dragging the bottom," she said helpfully.

I nodded. This wasn't really the time for a fishing lesson.

"Always gone there, he called it his sweet spot," she said. "Never didn't get a catch there, don't you know. For years. Then that summer, he kept pulling up stuff in the trawler—in the net. Stuff from that wreck." Another glance.

"Sands shift on the ocean floor, don't you know," she said. "Some things get covered, some things get uncovered."

"Okay," I said. "So he started finding artifacts from the Mignonette."

"He didn't know what it was called. He didn't do school much after eighth grade, didn't know all this history and stuff. Just knew what he was seeing. So he marked the coordinates and decided to see about it. Now he knew, it didn't matter if it got covered again, he'd be able to find it."

His retirement fund. "How was he planning on accessing it?"

She shook her head. "He wasn't," she said. "He didn't swim, himself, and he didn't have money for no fancy equipment. He was going to sell it, don't you know. The coordinates."

Something was coming together, but I still wasn't sure what it was. Something vague was finally taking shape. Behind me, John cleared his throat. "You have them coordinates?" he asked.

She shook her head. "No; Tony didn't want me involved," she said. "He didn't want it in my house, nor in his. He wanted me safe, and Sarah too."

"He had the coordinates on the Bessie G," I said.

She nodded.

"But that was years ago," I objected. "Anything that was written down has disintegrated by now."

The bright sparrow glance. "He carved the numbers on the inside of the ice-maker," she said simply.

She'd even asked me about it. The ice-maker. That bit of equipment no fishing boat is without, that keeps fish and shellfish fresh until they go to the refrigerated trucks waiting on the pier. The one thing Tony would always be able to count on. Not such a stupid move, that, I found myself thinking.

John got there before me. He whistled. "So that's why he was set on raising the Bessie G," he said.

I swiveled in my chair to face him. That made all the sense in the world, except… "How did he know?" I demanded. "How did Guy know the Mignonette's coordinates were in the Bessie G? And how did he even *find* the Bessie G?"

There was a moment of silence as we all thought about it. I tried again. "Helen. Tony had to have told someone else. Who else could he have talked to, besides you?"

She shook her head. "He wouldn't," she said. "He didn't even tell Sarah, don't you know."

This was so frustrating; every time I thought I had a hold of this thing it slithered out of my hands. Guy Husband was looking more and more like a villain, and Mirela's assessment of their relationship notwithstanding, I didn't want to see her get hurt.

And besides that, there was Pete. With all this going on, his murder—with a fish hook—had to tie in here somewhere.

"I don't know about you," I said, "but I think it's time to talk to Guy Husband."

18

The inn was almost nauseatingly cheery.

I still had Helen in tow and, curiously, John was also still with us. I hadn't quite figured out his interest in all of this, and as much as I liked the man, I had to confess to a fleeting suspicion running through my brain. John seemed to be a little too involved in all of this. Short of denying him entry into the Little Green Car, though, I didn't see how I could refuse him coming along, and so there he was.

There was another new face at reception, and I tried to find his name. Brad, Ben, Bill, one of those short male names. Couldn't find it. I smiled brightly and hoped he recognized me. "Is Guy Husband in? Can you ring his room?"

He recognized me. "Sydney. Glenn's been looking for you."

Another lurch in my stomach. I'd almost forgotten about the inn. "He hasn't been trying very hard," I said, fishing out my phone. "He didn't ca—oh. Right. Looks like he did." God only knew why the ringer was off. There was panic now, nibbling at the edges of my consciousness. I didn't want to hear what Glenn was going to tell me. *Breathe, Riley, just breathe.* "Guy Husband?" I asked again.

Bill or Ben or Brad nodded toward the guests' dining-room. "In there."

We trooped in. The inn was hopping; Bing Crosby was telling everyone about some little drummer boy, trees and lights were sparkling; cinnamon wafted on the air. The dining-room was a third full and it was only early afternoon.

Guy was sitting by the fireplace, a china cup and teapot at his elbow, and a plate of our pastry chef Angus' cranberry scones. My mouth was watering; I hadn't finished my lunch at the soup kitchen. He was reading the New York Times, which seemed, under the circumstances, ludicrously ordinary. I flopped into the armchair next to him, leaving Helen and John to fend for themselves. "Aren't you supposed to be out finding a pirate ship?"

He lowered the paper slowly. "Good afternoon to you, too, Sydney," he said coolly. "Won't you join me?"

"We need to talk," I informed him.

"Ah, straight to the point. Americans are so refreshingly direct." He took his time folding the newspaper. "How can I be of assistance today?"

"You know why we're here," I said. I wasn't quite sure how to articulate it myself.

He raised his eyebrows. "I can think off-hand of three or four reasons," he said. "Enlighten me."

John had pulled up a chair for Helen and now sat down on the ledge of the fireplace. His back was going to get very hot very quickly. Not my problem. I was still formulating a plan of attack when Helen leaned over and said, "Who told you my brother found your pirate ship?"

He looked at her. "Ms. Correia," he said after a moment. "I'm sure I don't know—"

John said, "Tell her."

We all looked at him. Maybe he wanted to get a move on so his back wouldn't burn; but there was something edgy and dangerous in his voice. Something that fit in with my lingering suspicions about his involvement.

"I say—"

John held up a hand. "It's too late," he said. "You can tell them, or I will."

Guy shook his head. "I don't think it's a very good—"

John cut him off. "I told him about it," he said. "Yeah, I found the coin on the back shore, like I told you, Sydney. But I already knew it was out there, and knew Tony had the coordinates." He glanced at Helen. "He told me," he said. "Tony and me, we went to school together. Yeah, so we'd drifted apart, what with his family and fishing and all, but we still saw each other at the OC." The Old Colony Tap, where not only did everybody know your name, they knew your parents' as well. It was that kind of place. "Tony, he never drank too much, don't think I ever saw him drunk, but he told me once. And he told me where."

"Why'd you never say anything?" Helen was looking at him as though he were a new fashion she wasn't sure was going to catch on.

John shrugged. "Why?" he asked. "What for? Who would I tell? When he showed up with that bullet in his head" —here Helen gave a little squeak— "well, I didn't need to be on no suspect list."

It made sense. "So why now?" I asked. "Why'd you contact Guy?"

"Look. Helen saw Tony leave port that night. But he couldn't have gone far, he couldn't have gotten out of the harbor."

"Why?"

He glanced at Guy. "You wouldn't know this," he said. "But all round the harbor and out into the bay, we got massive tides. Difference between low tide and high tide, it swallows some beaches."

That was true enough; I'd tried to go swimming once at low tide and felt like I was walking all the way to... "He went into the water at low tide!" I exclaimed.

John nodded. "He musta gone overboard when he got shot," he said. "But he wasn't dead. He walked to shore, an' that's why he died under the pilings there. I worked that out long ago."

"You never said," said Helen. There was nothing in her voice, no curiosity, no reproof. I thought she might be in shock.

John shrugged. "Police couldn't work that out, not doing their jobs," he said. "And no one was gonna drag the harbor for the Bessie G." That was true enough: we're the second-deepest natural harbor in the world. "But then, when that coin washed ashore, I remembered the guy I knew in Scotland, that he could find someone wanting to dive the wreck. And I could give him the key."

"Why?" I asked. "Why'd you want it raised?"

He looked at me with some astonishment. "Didn't you hear me? Tony and me, we was friends. Someone shot him. I thought maybe the answer was on the Bessie G. At the very least, they'd have to reopen the case, new evidence coming in." He took a deep breath and seemed to straighten up. "I wanted justice," he said.

As the end to a speech, it was effective as hell. There was a moment when the only sound was the fire crackling and Bing crooning.

And then, slowly, Guy began to clap his hands. Clap… pause… clap… pause. "Very nicely done," he said.

Helen looked at him, coldly. "A better motivation than you had," she said.

"My dear woman, I make no apologies for what I do," he said, an undercurrent of amusement in his voice.

"How did Robert Whittier find out?" I asked.

"Yes," said Guy. "I'd rather like to know that, myself."

John said, "I contacted him, too. No guarantees that one or the other would be interested. If I'd found five of you, I'd have told all five."

"So: mystery solved," said Guy languidly. He consulted his watch. "Sure you wouldn't like something to drink? Mirela will be joining me in a few minutes. We can make a tea party of it." He seemed to find the thought amusing.

Mirela… I didn't have time to think about her. She'd better not go back to Bulgaria. "I want to know what your plans are," I said to Guy.

The eyebrows, again. "My dear Sydney, I plan to lay claim to the Mignonette," he said. "I think I've been clear about that from the beginning. I have the coordinates in hand and tomorrow we'll take the Gargantua out. What happens then depends on the state of the wreck. If it's exploded…"

I held up a hand. I was suddenly feeling very tired. "I know, I know," I said. "You'll dive it if you can't raise it."

Helen said, "My brother's boat was just a means to an end for you. My sister-in-law, my nieces, they mean nothin'."

"My dear woman, I am pleased to be part of finding justice for them, but that is not my brief. We should be rejoicing, instead, that we both got something out of the endeavor."

John stood up. "So now it's in the hands of the police," he said. "That was the least I could do for him." He reached a hand to Helen. "Come on," he said. "Now we just have to wait. They'll release them for burying soon, I'm sure."

I turned to Guy. "Listen, if you know—"

Glenn's voice interrupted me. "Sydney."

There it went again, my stomach plunging south. No. I didn't want to know. Please don't tell me. I took a deep breath and turned slowly. "I'd like to see you in my office, if you have a minute." He looked tired and harried and I so didn't want to hear what he had to say.

John said, "We can get a taxi, Sydney, you go ahead." Guy was already reaching, languidly, for his newspaper. *Breathe, Riley.* "Coming," I said to Glenn.

He seemed enormous behind the desk. There aren't many desks in the world that could stand up to Glenn, stature-wise, come to think of it. Which I was, because I was trying desperately not to think about why I was there. "Looks like Christmas is well in hand," he remarked.

I swallowed and slid into the guest chair in front of him. "It looks perfect," I said miserably. He was going to sell. I just knew he was going to sell. Next year, let's see what a hotel chain's cost-cutting measures would do to the Race Point's extravagant Holly Folly and winter décor and celebrations.

Everything would change. Adrienne, our diva chef, would have to go; I couldn't see her allowing anyone to dictate either her meals or her budget. Martin, the maître d' in the restaurant, he'd probably leave too. It wouldn't be the same. It would never be the same.

And me? What else could I do? None of the other establishments in town was large enough to employ a wedding planner/event organizer. I wasn't altogether sure that the Race Point was, either; Barry had clearly created the position for me. I'd have to work for the new company… or leave Provincetown.

I couldn't leave Provincetown.

"I've been going over the numbers," said Glenn. He waited until I finally looked up and met his eyes. "It makes all the sense in the world to sell."

I took a deep breath to speak, but he held up his hand. "And you know I never wanted to be an innkeeper," he said. "It's been tempting." He drummed his fingers on the edge of the desk. "But what we have here, it's more than a business. Barry built a family. I can't in good faith let numbers change that."

I stared at him. "You're not selling?"

"There will be some changes," he said, as though he hadn't heard me. "You and Mike, I want you to take on more responsibility. I want to travel some. I don't want to be tied down here all the time. I want to learn to ski."

Ski? Glenn? He'd look at home with all the real bears on the mountainside, I found myself thinking, even as the realization and the happiness tricked through my brain. "You're not selling," I said again, and this time it wasn't a question. "Glenn!"

"I'm not selling. I want us to do some planning and reorganization after New Year's. But I'm keeping the inn."

"Glenn!" Before he could stop me I was around the desk and hugging him. "Glenn, Glenn, Glenn!"

"All right, all right," he said, trying to disengage my arms.

"Glenn! I love you!"

"All right," he said again, and this time succeeded in moving me away from him. "Enough of that."

"I thought bears were cuddly." In my relief, I pushed it a little, wondering how he'd take it, and to my astonishment he burst out laughing. "Go on, get out of here. You must have a tree to trim or something."

"They're all trimmed. Glenn, you are a rock star."

"Go away," said the rock star.

***

I felt exhilarated, like I'd suddenly gotten a new lease on life. I'd imagined the worst and it hadn't come to pass. I was on top of the world. I was over the moon. Name your cliché, and I was feeling it.

The cold bit me as I left the inn, too excited to sit still. The mysteries of the Mignonette and the Bessie G could wait. Barry's inn—no, *Glenn's* inn—was safe. I didn't even mind the cold. I wanted to laugh and dance and touch the stars. Pity it was daytime and I couldn't see any.

I walked all the way down MacMillan Pier. The Gargantua was gone, presumably following the directions Tony had scratched in his ice-maker to the pots of pirate treasure. I hoped that Guy would have the heart and the sense to give some of it to Helen, or to set up a memorial, or something.

But now? Now I was just enjoying being alive in Provincetown.

I stood for a few minutes looking out at the cormorants and gulls clustered on the breakwater. The sun was moving toward the west, the short winter day starting to give up its ghost. A door slammed behind me and Craig came over from the harbormaster's office. "Hey, Sydney."

"Hey, Craig."

He stood next to me, looking out at the harbor, sharing the moment. "It's good to be alive," he said at last.

"No," I said. "It's freaking *great* to be alive."

He clapped me on the back. "Want some coffee? I just made a pot."

"Sure, why not?" I followed him into the office, my eyes and nose streaming from the cold. "I don't know how they all do it," I said, perching on one of the bar stools in front of the counter.

"Who? Do what? Do you take sugar?"

"The fishermen," I said, gesturing vaguely out the windows surrounding us. "It's freezing cold here, it must be so much worse out there." I shivered and turned back. "Two sugars, please." I knew that as soon as my excitement about the inn died down I'd need the sugar high.

"They're used to it," he said, going back to my remark. "A lot of people would hate your job, too."

"Not me," I said cheerfully. "Fulltime wedding consultant, part-time sleuth. Except I haven't been doing too well in the sleuthing department."

He came over and set the two steaming mugs on the counter. "Watch out, that's hot. Why, what are you trying to find out?"

"Well, no one's closer to finding out who shot Tony Correia, and who killed Pete," I said. "We've all been running around dazzled by pirate treasure, but they're what really matters, aren't they? Oh, and not just Tony, now it's Tony's family, too. All of them."

"The police have any leads?"

I wrapped my hands around my cup. "Hey, you'd know that better than I do. You're part of the investigation, aren't you?" Nearly everything in a seaside town involves the harbormaster at one level or another.

Craig shrugged. "Roger is, maybe," he conceded. "Not my pay grade."

"I just feel like there's a missing piece, something that's right under my nose and I'm just not seeing," I said, finally taking a sip of coffee. "Like they're all tied together. It's too much of a coincidence that Pete got killed just at the same time that Guy arrives to raise the Bessie G, doesn't it? He must have known something." I shook my head. "I didn't know him that well, I don't know who he hung out with, so it's hard to figure out who he must have been a threat to."

Craig sipped his coffee, his eyes out the window, watching the harbor. No matter what else is happening around them, they're always doing that, scanning. Just like regular cops. Never off-duty, never not watchful. I felt a sudden surge of gratitude. I drank some more coffee. "I feel like at some level all I've done is muddle things up," I said. "Did you know Pete was killed with a fish hook?"

He nodded. "Heard that."

"Not everybody can handle one of those," I said. "Not everybody even knows what one is."

"This is P'town," he reminded me. "A lot of folks do."

"It has to be tied in," I said again. "You know, if he'd been knifed or beaten or maybe even shot, it could have been an argument got out of hand." These things happened. Maybe not as much as in the days when Norman Mailer was alive and got into drunken brawls with the men of the fishing community; but it still happened. "But a fish hook? Cripes, Craig, you have to plan that."

"Not if the fight's on a boat," he said conversationally. "A fish hook's the first thing to hand."

I reached over and touched his arm. "I'm sorry. I shouldn't be talking about this. Pete was your friend. You must miss him. You must be devastated."

He nodded and I left it for the moment. Drank my coffee. Felt deliciously warm and sleepy. "You guys always keep the heat up like this? No wonder our taxes are so high." My voice sounded oddly like it was coming at me from far away.

The truth was, all I really wanted to do was put my head down on the counter and take a nap. Just a small nap.

Just for a few minutes.

19

I was very far from warm.

Consciousness returned, slowly and painfully, and the first thing I noticed was the cold. And the dark. And the throbbing pulse of a motor somewhere. It took me another few moments to realize it was very close to me.

That I was on a boat. A boat moving through the December waters of Cape Cod Bay. This couldn't be good news, not on any level.

And the cold was intense.

I tried moving, an a flaming pain shot through me, so I stopped that right away. My head was throbbing to a different rhythm than the engine noise, and add to all that, of course, was the fear. And just a little *déjà vu*. The last time I'd been knocked out and come to, it had been in time for me and Thea to almost get killed. That didn't exactly bode well for the current situation.

The current situation. I tried fuzzily to re-construct it. What had I been doing before set-ting out on this December jaunt at sea?

I'd been at the harbormaster's office. Drink-ing coffee. *Stupid, stupid girl.* There'd been some-thing in that coffee besides coffee. And Craig had put it there.

I moved at the thought and the same sharp pain jabbed at my side and I groaned. Rather loudly. Well, as much as I'd *like* to think I can take all these adventures in stride, at heart I'm still a coward. Not the strong silent type at all.

Someone said something indistinguishable and the engine slowed down. A moment later the noise subsided, a light was snapped on, and Craig appeared, looking anxious.

I was in the cabin of a motorboat, no doubt one of the ones run by the harbormaster crew. I wasn't tied up, but that didn't particularly mat-ter as my limbs had all the strength of wet noo-dles. Whatever he'd given me, it was effective.

"Sydney," said Craig. He looked—of all things—concerned.

I opened my mouth to say something no doubt pithy and clever, but nothing came out but a croak.

"Here, wait," he said, and fished around somewhere out of my field of vision, returning with a cup of water. "Drink this."

He held it to my mouth and I gulped it down. "What the hell, Craig?"

He was looking distressed. "I'd hoped you wouldn't wake up," he said.

I didn't have to ask what he meant; what he meant was all too clear. The fact that he'd wanted to do it with the least muss and fuss didn't reassure me—if anything, it somehow added to the claw of fear trying to tear up my stomach. "Why do you have to do it?" I asked. I didn't think I needed to be any more specific.

He eased me back until I was more or less comfortable in the captain's chair. I gripped the arms as hard as I could, but my own arms were doing the wet-noodle thing again and it was a little beyond my current capabilities.

Craig sat down across from me. I could see now we were in a small cabin, just behind the galley that nestled in the bow. A detached part of my brain congratulated me on coming up with that bit of nautical lore. I was about to die, but damn it, I knew the bow from the stern. There must be a table that could be fitted in between us; right now it was just open floorspace. He leaned forward partly across the space between us. "I didn't mean for it to happen like this," he said, his voice sounding very young and very earnest.

"I'm relieved to hear it."

If he heard the sarcasm he didn't give any indication of it. "It's all just gone so wrong, and I didn't know how to get it back," he said. So rational. "At first it was all about the wreck, and selling off the coordinates," he said. "We were going to do an auction, you know? Sell them to the highest bidder." A pause. "Sick of life on the Cape, working for all the rich people. Watching them come in every year, take over the town. Greedy bastards, treating townsfolk like dirt. Throw their garbage everywhere, act like it's theirs to do whatever they want with. Tired of telling them how welcome they were, when I just want to kill them all. Get things back the way they used to be. That's all I really wanted. If I can't get it here, I can leave, get it somewhere else. Be one of the people who own things, who own places." Another pause; he seemed to be thinking it over. He looked up at me again. "You see, don't you, Sydney? It's just about money, you know?"

He seemed to be waiting for a response, so I nodded.

A quick breath. "I know it's too late for that now," he said. "Never even got them coordinates, so there's no auction. It's over, it's been over." He scratched his head. "But now? It's just about not going to jail, now."

I nodded. It hurt. I wondered what he'd given me, what was in that coffee. "Because of Pete," I said. "You killed Pete. I don't get that part. Why? You guys were close."

"It wasn't as bad as you think," he said. "Pete was dying. No one knew but me, not yet, but he had prostate cancer. It's one of the worst, you know. He didn't have a chance."

"So it doesn't matter that you took away the time he had? That's almost *worse*, Craig."

He shook his head. "He'd have preferred it," he said.

"Did you give him the chance to choose?"

He didn't answer. He was looking down at his hands. It occurred to me, with some surprise, that he was serious. That he hadn't really wanted to do this. That circumstances had pushed him and he thought he didn't have choices. It was a narrow assessment of the situation, but that didn't make it any less understandable. "He wouldn't listen to me," he said, a little desperately. "I wouldn't've had to do it if he'd listened to me."

My brain still wasn't at a hundred percent. "Listened to you about what?"

"That we'd missed our chance," he said. He looked up at me then. "By the time the English guy got here, it was too late. But Pete wouldn't let go. He had plans for the money. We were just biding our time till we could find where Tony put the coordinates. We'd searched his place, first thing, top to bottom. Pete even tried to get close to Helen for a while to see what she knew, but she wasn't having any of it. I told him to give up. We weren't gonna find them. But he didn't want to let go."

"Why didn't you think of that," I asked, "before you shot Tony?"

"That was a mistake, too," he said, quickly. "You gotta believe me, Sydney, that was a mistake." Yeah, right, along with whatever other mistake was about to overtake me.

The longer he talked, the longer I stayed alive. "How do you shoot someone by mistake?"

"Pete was waving the gun around," he said. Of course it would be Pete; easy to blame the dead guy. "Listen, it just all went wrong. We saw him go out that night, same as usual. We went after him in the harbor, put on the lights to stop him, boarded the boat. We thought we'd just pressure him for the coordinates. To find the pirate treasure." He sounded like a little boy.

"How did you know he had them?"

He looked at me as though I were mad. "He told us. He told a whole bunch of us one night down the OC. He probably didn't remember; don't think any of them remembered, we were doing shooters. Pete and me, we remembered."

"And why would he give them to you?"

He flushed; embarrassment. "We're law enforcement," he said finally. "We coulda made it difficult for him. He had to get out every day to make a living. We coulda…" His voice trailed off.

"So you blackmailed your friend."

"Didn't matter," Craig said. "He wasn't gonna go along with it anyway. And Pete was just waving the gun around to try and intimidate him, and—"

"Wait," I said. "What about Sarah? What about the girls?"

"We didn't know they was there," he said, simply.

I stared at him. It had all been so innocent, after all, just a night outing, one that happened on the wrong night. The hazards of life. The crapshoot that allows one to live and another to die.

Craig was still talking. "They was down below, and the hatch was closed," he said. "They was making a picnic dinner." He swallowed, hard; this was difficult for him. In spite of myself, I felt a little sorry for him.

Just a little.

"So Pete shoots Tony by accident," I said. "Then what happened?"

"He went over the side," said Craig. "We dint know he was still alive. I think he probably thought we'd bring the Bessie G back. And we were gonna, too, just say we'd found her abandoned in the outer harbor, tow her in to Mac-Millan, but then I heard one of the girls laughing." He looked away. "I keep hearing her," he said. "It wakes me up at night, the sound of her laughing. I can't get it out of my head."

Serves you right, I thought; but all I said was, "what happened?"

He shrugged. "What do you think happened? We locked the hatch and motored the boat out a ways and opened the seacocks. Got back on ours and headed back to the harbor.

I forgot trying to be gentle with him. "You left them locked in the cabin to drown!" It wasn't a question.

Craig nodded, miserable. "I didn't mean for it to happen," he said. "You don't know how many times I wished I could go back and do that over again. You don't know how much I've had to drink to stop hearing them."

"You'll forgive me," I said drily, "if I'm not too sympathetic about your insomnia."

That brought his focus back to me with a click I could almost hear. *Bad move, Riley.* "Helen shouldn't have talked to you," he said suddenly, almost savagely. "You wouldn't have figured it out."

"I didn't figure it out, Craig," I said, a little desperately. "If you hadn't told me what you just told me, I'd never—" I stopped, looking at him in horror.

"You were gonna," he said. "Come on, Sydney, I've seen you in action. You act like the town's a background for your murder mysteries."

"That's not fair," I said. "I love this town. I've just—it's I can't leave a puzzle alone. And sometimes it's been about people I care about…"

"You didn't have to meet Helen," he said. "You didn't have to do this." His voice was gaining strength; he was convincing himself. "This isn't my fault."

"Why Pete?" I asked, trying to distract him. I didn't have a plan other than to buy myself a few more minutes of life. "Why'd you kill Pete?"

"Pete was an idiot," said Craig. "He was my friend, an' all, but he was still an idiot. That English guy comes here with all his money, and Craig thinks he can still sell him something. He told him he had the coordinates." He shook his head. "Stupid. Was gonna take a down payment and then take off. But by then the Bessie G's stern had washed up. It was too late. He was gonna land us in jail."

"A fish hook?"

"We have 'em on all our fleet. And Pete and me, we're out together a lot. I was gonna just tip him overboard."

I felt a little sick. "You killed him *here*?"

"Where else?" He sounded genuinely curious. "Even in the wintertime, you know it as well as anybody, you're never all alone in town. Someone would see. I'd had enough of being scared all the time." And that's why he thought I had to die: so he wouldn't be scared all the time.

"So how'd he end up on the pier?"

"Storm," he said. "Remember, just before the lobster pot tree lighting, they was talking about a nor'easter?"

"Vaguely," I said. "It stayed offshore." Nothing had tainted the town's festivities, I thought. Well, except for that one little murder.

"Yeah, well, it was like summertime out in the Bay that night, busy as hell, cargo ship coming in to shelter, Coast Guard all over the place. And once I thought about it… Pete had his share of problems. He drank too much and he played cards too much. Easy to imagine someone doing him for a bad debt." He shrugged. "So I waited until everyone was down at the lighting and dragged him up and left him. Didn't know you'd be the one to find him."

"He was your *friend*," I said.

"I'm not going to jail," he said simply. "I got a brother, he's in super-max up to Shirley. I know what happens there, what they do to you. Not a chance I could take." He paused. "It were the other way around, Pete wouldn't have hesitated."

Tell yourself that and see if it helps you sleep. I couldn't imagine how he dealt with the rest of it. The Bessie G, and the screams as it went down. How he'd slept at all since then was beyond me. Hell, I hadn't done it, I'd just been told about it, and I already knew that just knowing was going to give me nightmares.

If I lived long enough to have any, that was.

It seemed impolitic to bring his attention back to the here and now, but that cabin wasn't heated and I was pretty sure my fingers were starting to get frostbite. *It won't take long,* said a voice in my head, coming from a long distance away. *No one survives in that water for more than a few minutes. You won't feel much.*

Craig stood up abruptly. "Gotta get back," he said. "I'm sorry, Sydney." He reached over and grabbed my elbow and helped me stand up. "This wasn't what I meant to have happen," he said. "You weren't supposed to wake up. I didn't mean for this to happen." *No, you never meant for any of it to happen.*

"And yet here we are," I said. Eye level with him. With Craig, one of the nicest guys in town. With Craig, the killer.

If I didn't do something, I was going to die. It really was that simple. So I did what anyone would do. I kneed him, sharply, in the groin, and when he let go of my arm I flew up the stairs for the controls.

Turns out I don't know much about motorboats. Well, any kind of boat. Thea and I sometimes rent a small sailboat from Flyer's in the summer and go skidding around the harbor, but that's the extent of my nautical know-how. Perhaps living in a seaside town I should have known more, should have done better. As it was, I was nonplussed by the array of options on the dashboard. It probably wasn't even called a dashboard.

Behind me, Craig was still bent over. I had a few more moments to save myself. I kept pressing buttons and an occasional light came on, but no engines roared to life. I looked out over the harbor, and saw nothing—only the Pilgrim Monument, festively adorned for the season, all bright and cheery. Somewhere over there, people were sitting in warm rooms drinking hot cider. I stabbed desperately at some more buttons, and banged on a lever or two. No sense in being delicate now. If I broke something, fine.

The sound came at me first, in a roar, and for a split second all I could think was that it was a rogue wave. Or a whale. Or something big and horrible and undefined. My brain wasn't exactly in its happy place. Then the searchlight snapped on and a voice came over a loudspeaker as the helicopter hovered over us. "Harbormaster! This is the Coast Guard! Prepare to be boarded!"

Craig was pulling himself up the stairway—or whatever the nautical equivalent was—and was heading straight for the controls. I've been in that position before, someone holding me who wishes me very much ill indeed, and I wasn't playing that game again; I moved across the deck faster than the favorite in a five-k race. There was a ladder snaking down from the helicopter now and everything was a frightening sharp white and there was nothing but the sound of the rotors, and I shut my eyes and slid down to the deck and grabbed the railing and hung on for dear life.

When I opened them again, someone was pulling me up and for a split second I thought it was Craig, but this was a young woman. "Are you all right, ma'am?"

I looked around wildly. "Where—" There was no one else on the deck.

"Divers are in the water," she said quietly. "Come below." And I allowed her to lead me back down the stairs and sat still while she wrapped a blanket around me. The engines came back on. There were a couple other people on board and one of them thrust something hot into my hands. "Drink that."

My teeth were chattering against the rim of the thermos cup. "How did you know where we were?" I asked. If ever there were a *deus ex machina*, this was it.

"Detective Agassi," she said. She said something else, but I couldn't hear it, there was too much noise. Julie must have reached some sort of conclusion about Craig on her own. She'd tell me, in time. Or not.

All I could feel, now, was the cold. And thinking about Craig, who wouldn't have wanted to be saved.

I hoped I'd been right about the way you died at sea. I hoped it had been relatively painless. Because, despite everything, I still liked him.

20

Mirela was being protective. "No one can see her," she announced, standing in the doorway of the Race Point Inn's lounge.

The normalcy of the whole thing was disconcerting. It was still, somehow, Holly Folly. Greed and violence and betrayal could be happening out at sea, but in Provincetown, nothing was going to change the sheer joy of Holly Folly. The Boston Gay Men's Chorus was performing in another hour. Usually I attended the concert.

I was currently otherwise employed.

People were drifting about the rest of the inn, laughing and chatting, cups of eggnog in their hands. Music was playing, trees were twinkling. Nothing could be more normal than Holly Folly, and—somehow—nothing could be more jarring, either.

I'd had to answer a lot of questions—from the Coast Guard, from the police, and from a scandalized Roger the harbormaster. I couldn't imagine what he was going through. Pete and Craig's betrayal must be killing him. The office was going to echo with their absence for a long time, their ghosts wraiths dancing on the pier when the mist came up.

But I didn't have a whole lot of energy to devote to feeling sorry for anybody. Before I was even finished with officialdom's questions, an EMT was checking me out, shining a light into my eyes and reading my pulse; I was, apparently, borderline hypothermic. That might have explained why I felt I was drifting so much, my sentences ragged, losing my way as I tried to talk. It was as if I was meandering my way through several dimensions with no focus and no will to focus.

Finally they gave up and someone gave me a ride to the inn, where there was a whole committee waiting. Thea, who didn't trust anyone but herself to check me over and pronounce me alive and well. Mirela, who had appointed herself my protector and gatekeeper. And, surprisingly, Guy.

He was the one who told me. Once I was ensconced in a deep armchair by the fire, wearing someone's sweat pants and an oversized Coast Guard sweatshirt, my hands around yet another hot drink, Guy came in and sat near me. "We found her," he said.

"Who?" For one terrible moment I thought he was talking about a person.

"The Mignonette," he said. "Thanks to the Correias, and you, we found her. She's in decent shape. If we can't raise her, then for sure we can dive her come summer."

"And you beat Robert Whittier," I said.

He smiled. "There's that," he acknowledged. "But I wanted to tell you—we're setting up a memorial to the family. And a college scholarship in their name. Helen suggested it. Something for a kid from P'town. It was the best we could do."

Mirela came in then and sat next to him and without either of them looking at the other, their hands found each other, fingers entwining. So that was still a thing. I was happy for them, actually. Staring death in the face gives you a sense of perspective. Anyone who can find any bit of happiness, I say, go for it.

I still wondered what sixth sense made Mirela paint her images of the Correias' last moments. And how she was going to sleep from now on, for the rest of her life, with them still in her head.

Mike came in, distracted and anxious. He'd once fished me out of the harbor, so he had to have been experiencing at least a little déjà vu. "Sydney. Thank God. Are you sure you're all right?"

"I'm sure." I gave him my most reassuring smile. "Go away, you have work to do."

He went away, but made sure Adrienne the diva chef had some food sent in to us, and later,

I didn't know how much later, he came back. "There's a call for you on the house phone," he said.

I made a face. I'd been snoozing and was warm and comfortable. "Do I have to? Can you take a message?"

He pulled the landline extension over and handed it to me. "Trust me, you want to," he said.

I took the receiver. "Hello? This is Sydney."

"So it is," said the one voice I wanted to hear. "You're a difficult woman to reach, *cara signorina*."

Ali.

"It's absurd, the way you use Italian," I said, ridiculously pleased. "Are you all right? Are you done?"

"Done; I wound it all up yesterday morning, and I'm far more all right than you apparently are, babe, if what Mike's been telling me is anything to go by." A slight pause. "Are you really? All right?"

I snuggled farther down into the cushions, smiling idiotically. "I am now," I said. "Hearing your voice is the best medicine. Oh, I'm so glad you're all right. I've been... well, never mind how I've been." I paused, imagining him at the airport in Los Angeles or San Francisco. Wherever he was. "How soon can you get here?"

"If Mirela will let me in the room, in about thirty seconds."

"Ali!" I shrieked, up and out of the chair. They were both standing in the doorway, Mirela and Ali, and my heart felt like it would burst. I threw off the comforter I'd had around me and ran for it, nearly knocking him over in the process. "Ali, Ali, Ali…"

He swung me around and we enjoyed a rather long kiss. "I can't believe you're here," I said. "I've been so worried." Understatement of the century. God, and he looked good, still doing the designer stubble on his chin, his dark eyes luminous. A little dangerous, and more gorgeous even than I remembered.

The same couldn't, of course, be said for me. But I had a good excuse for my dishevelment. This time, anyway.

"*Cara*," he kept saying. "I love you, I love you, I love you." *What I tell you three times is true.*

Behind him, Mirela made a show of clearing her throat. "Er, sunshine, this is not your only surprise," she said. I disengaged from Ali enough to look past him, over his shoulder, to see her. "Why, what's up?" It couldn't get any better, I thought, than this present perfect wonderful moment. What new delight could possibly be in store?

Mirela stepped to one side and I heard the voice before I saw her. "And she'd better not take an attitude with me, is all I can say. I don't need her to take an attitude."

Oh, hell. I'd forgotten about it altogether. My mother wasn't just coming; my mother was here.

Breathe, Riley. Just breathe.

Acknowledgments

So many people help, inspire, and shepherd a book from the first idea to the printed page. My deepest gratitude goes to Arthur Mahoney of HomePort Press, for his courage, insight, and friendship. I treasure all three.

My thanks go as always to all the beautiful people of Provincetown, who generously allow me to use so many of their own special selves in my books. Any errors in their portrayal are mine.

To those who contribute in myriad ways to the creation of a Sydney story: Colin Kegler, Pat Medina (for road trips and plot ideas), Mark Cortale, Chip Capelli (who hasn't missed a single event, and with my apologies), Michael Ponestowski, Freddy Biddle, Margo Nash (for everything, but especially for being my guinea-pig First Reader), Carem Bennett, Corinne Diana, Shelley Kenigsberg, Dianne Kopser, Bob Allen, Julie & Katy Blackburn, Michelle Crone, Anastasia & Sydnia Czarnecki (my lovely family), and Tony, Suzanne, and Albert Rodrigues (for all the Portuguese food, and especially the laughter). To Nini Lyons and Avis Johnson, for your patience. And to Sister Kathryn, for always pointing me in the right direction.

Thanks to Deborah Karacozian, Nan Cinnater, and Clayton Nottleman for so energetically being my emissaries at the Provincetown Bookshop, to Jeff Peters at East End Books, and to Miladinka Milic for Sydney's amazing cover designs. And to Kyre Song, who is so much more than just my web guy.

Thanks to Erin for her tireless editing. Any mistakes that remain here are mine, not hers. To the ladies from Jungle Red Writers for their support and inspiration. And to the New England chapter of the Sisters in Crime—well, for sisterhood!

My gratitude goes out to you all, and to anyone I might have inadvertently left out, for sometimes I am a bear of very little brain. No, not that kind of bear.

Author's Note

As with all the Sydney Riley mysteries, there's an element of truth hidden within the fiction. The Whydah was indeed pirate Black Sam Bellamy's flagship and went down in a storm on its way from the Caribbean to Maine. The ship is real; "Robert Whittier" is not. The wreck was discovered by renowned underwater archaeologist Barry Clifford. As of this writing, it is the only the only fully-authenticated wreck of a Golden Age pirate ship. Clifford and his team continue to find treasure, though not just the kind we generally associate with pirate ships; this treasure enriches our understanding of the past and the people who lived in it. When you come to Cape Cod, be sure to visit the museums that display the team's findings and that put them in context.

Provincetown has a number of very nice and very competent harbormasters. They control docking arrangements for the ferries, the whale watch boats, the commercial fishing fleet, the recreational charter fleet, and the cruise ships. They're responsible for all marine traffic in and out of the harbor and perform the difficult communication with Portuguese fishermen, the LGBTQ community, scientists, squid fishermen, and others who use the pier and harbor. These men and women work year-round making sure the harbor runs safely and smoothly, but in no way are Roger, Craig, or Pete based on any of them.

Oddly enough, it's true that many fishermen do not know how to swim. This is the Atlantic Ocean, with hypothermia minutes away once you hit the water. Most of them say it's just easier to let it happen. It's one of those myriad things you don't think about until you spend time with the people who have to.

I live in Provincetown and try to portray the town as clearly and correctly as I can (well, minus the murders, anyway!). Any errors in this series are my own.

About The Author

Bestselling author Jeannette de Beauvoir writes mystery and historical fiction (and often books at the intersection of the two) that uncover dark secrets and hidden truths, and explore a sense of connection to place.

A Book Sense Book-of-the-Year finalist, she's a member of the Authors Guild, the Mystery Writers of America, Sisters in Crime, and the National Writers Union.

Her delight is to find characters true to the spaces in which they live. She herself lives and writes in a cottage in Provincetown, on Cape Cod, Massachusetts, and loves the collection of people who assemble at a place like Land's End.

Find out more, and read her blog, at jeannettedebeauvoir.com.

Did You Enjoy This Book?

If you did, please…

1)**share your opinion** on Goodreads, and/or Amazon;

2)**visit my Amazon page** and check out some of my other books;

3)give the book a boost; **tell people about** it on Facebook and Twitter;

4)**subscribe to my newsletter** at **jeannettedebeauvoir.com** for book reviews, short stories, quizzes, free stuff, previews of upcoming work, and more;

5)ask your local bookseller **to stock** Sydney Riley books;

6) make them your **choice for your next book club** meeting (I'll even join you by Skype or Zoom if you'd like me to!);

7) **email me** at jeannettedebeauvoir@gmail.com;

8) and **watch for** the next Sydney Riley mystery from Homeport Press!